Louis Armstrong

Young Music Maker

Illustrated by Al Fiorentino

Louis Armstrong

Young Music Maker

Aladdin Paperbacks

First Aladdin Paperbacks edition 1997
Copyright © 1972 by the Bobbs-Merrill Company, Inc.

Aladdin Paperbacks
An imprint of Simon & Schuster
Children's Publishing Division
1230 Avenue of the Americas
New York, NY 10020

10 9 8 7 6 5 4 3 2 1

Library of Congress Cataloging-in-Publication Data

Millender, Dharathula H.
Louis Armstrong : young music maker / by Dharathula H. Millender ;
illustrated by Al Fiorentino.
p.   cm. — (Childhood of famous Americans)
Originally published: Indianapolis : Bobbs-Merrill, 1972.
Summary: A biography of a trumpeter of humble origin who received international acclaim as a jazz entertainer.
ISBN 0-689-80881-X (pbk.)
1. Armstrong, Louis, 1900–1971—Juvenile literature.   2. Jazz musicians—
United States—Biography—Juvenile literature.
[1. Armstrong, Louis, 1900–1971. 2. Musicians. 3. Afro-Americans—
Biography.] I. Fiorentino, Al, ill. II. Title. III. Series: Childhood of
Famous Americans series.
ML3930.A75M6   1997
781.65'092—dc20
96-24544
CIP AC MN

Dedicated to:
Mrs. Manuella Duplessis Jones (Captain
Joseph Jones's widow)
Mrs. Beatrice Armstrong Collins (Mama
Lucy)

Special thanks to:
Mr. O. C. W. Taylor; Pat Wynn, Dixieland Hall, New Orleans; Jazz Museum; Richard B. Allen, Archive of New Orleans Jazz, Tulane University Library; John E. Morehiser, Jr., Supervisor of Planning, New Orleans Public Schools; Files of the *Louisiana Weekly*, New Orleans; Files of the *Chicago Defender;* Henry C. Hastings, Head, Reference Department, Gary Public Library; Mrs. Manuella Duplessis Jones, widow of Captain Joseph Jones; Mrs. Beatrice Armstrong Collins (Mama Lucy); and the late Lil Hardin Armstrong

Numerous smaller illustrations

Contents

Louis Armstrong

Young Music Maker

A New Baby on
James Alley

It was the Fourth of July, 1900, on James Alley in New Orleans. The air was thick with the sounds of people celebrating on the street. Everyone was making noise and having fun. Soon two men started an argument and faced each other, ready to fight. Willie Armstrong left his mother's house and stepped outside. Inside the house his wife Mayann was about ready to give birth to her first child.

Willie tried to quiet the crowd. He stepped into the group where the two angry men were having an argument. Suddenly one of the men reached in his pocket for a weapon.

The crowd screamed and moved back a little. Calmly Willie put his hands on the two angry men and tried to separate them. "This is no way to celebrate the Fourth of July, fellows," he said pleadingly. "Why do you want to fight and kill each other? Besides, my wife's about ready to have a baby inside the house."

The two men stopped arguing, and the people crowded around Willie to ask questions. "So you're about to become a father," said a woman. "Which do you want, a boy or a girl?"

"A boy, of course," replied Willie proudly.

He turned to go back into the house but paused briefly to glance at the two angry men. "Don't start to argue or fight again, fellows," he cautioned. "I don't want to have to attend a funeral after the birth of a son."

"Now just who said you will have a son, Willie?" asked a man in the crowd. Then everybody started to laugh and jabber loudly.

12

Inside the house Willie went over to his young wife and kissed her. His mother, Josephine Armstrong, looked up from washing the dishes and said, "It won't be long now."

A friend, Miss Sally, had come to the house to serve as a midwife. Many people in those days had a midwife to take the place of a doctor when babies were born. All Black babies and most white babies were born at home. There was no hospital for Black people in New Orleans at that time.

Before long the noise outside began to build up again. Once more the two men began to argue in front of the house. Their voices grew louder and louder. "Go stop them from arguing again, son," said Willie's mother, "and stay out for a while to keep them quiet."

Just as Willie stepped outside there was the sharp crack of pistols. The bitter argument had ended in a shooting scrape. The two men had killed each other. At once the people in the street became quiet as they stood staring at the two dead bodies on the pavement.

The Fourth of July was a big holiday in New Orleans. People knew it was our country's birthday and they wanted to celebrate in some way or other. Almost everyone celebrated by singing, shouting, or just making noise. Some, like the two dead men, just had to get wild.

Willie and Mayann Armstrong lived in Willie's mother's home, which was tiny but neat and clean. It was located on a little street only a block long, called James Alley. This street was in a crowded section, called Back 'o Town.

All kinds of people, including many children, lived on crowded James Alley. The houses were small and built close together, and people moved in wherever they could find a place to sleep. Scattered here and there between the houses there were several bars and saloons.

The tiny Armstrong house, which contained only one room, was very crowded. There were single beds in two corners of the room and a double bed in a third corner. The other corner included a stove and a table with chairs. The furniture and stove took up most of the space, so there was scarcely any room to move about.

The little crowded room was very clean. There was no carpet or rug on the wooden floor, but it glistened from being swept and scrubbed to keep it clean. The Armstrong family always was sweeping, scrubbing, or dusting.

After Willie watched the bodies of the two men carted off to the morgue, he turned to go back into the house. Just as he reached the door, he heard a baby cry inside the house. He took hold of the doorknob but found the door locked. Then he turned to the people still on the street and cried, "My son has been born!"

People came flocking from everywhere to

celebrate with him. They wanted to go inside
the house to see the new baby. "Let us go in
with you," said a friendly old woman. "We want
to see your new son."

16

Willie dropped his hands helplessly. "I can't get in myself," he said.

"What do you mean, you can't get in?" asked another woman. "We want to see your son."

At this moment an elderly lady in the crowd tried to calm everyone. "Just wait," she said. "Willie's mother or Miss Sally will open the door to let us know when we can come in."

The people in the crowd groaned, but waited patiently. Soon Willie's mother opened the door and appeared, holding a little bundle in her arms. "You have a son, Willie," she said calmly. "Here, take him in your arms."

"Did you hear what Mama said, folks?" cried Willie gleefully. "I have a son! I told you the baby would be a boy!"

Willie took the new baby and cradled him gently in his arms. The people in the crowd moved forward to get a good look at the baby. "Congratulations, Willie," they said.

Soon Willie turned with the new baby in his arms and went inside the house. The members of the crowd moved away on tiptoe and remained quiet the rest of the day. They let the new mother and baby have peace and quiet.

Willie's father, William Armstrong, and his mother, Josephine, had been married after a brief courtship on a steamboat. William, whom everybody called Will, had obtained a job working in the boiler room of a steamboat that traveled between New Orleans and Biloxi, Mississippi. Most of his work had consisted of tossing pieces of firewood and sometimes chunks of coal into the furnace.

To help pass the time on the boat, Will had entertained the other workers by singing songs and telling stories. Often he had acted out the songs by going through all sorts of contortions. Finally when he had become tired, he had slumped into a seat in a corner and sung.

"I gotta home in-a dat rock . . . Don't you
    see . . . Don't you see?
I gotta home in-a dat rock . . . Don't you
    see . . . Don't you see?
When dat last trumpet sounds, and they
    lay poor Will in dat ground,
I'll be resting in-a dat rock . . . Don't you
    see . . . Don't you see?"

Josephine had worked on the steamboat as a maid to help look after the cabins. She had been born on a cotton plantation not far from New Orleans. As a young lady she had been of small stature but a bundle of energy.

One day Will had happened to meet Josephine, and a few weeks later they had been married. Then they had settled in New Orleans.

Will soon had obtained a job working on the New Orleans levee. He had handled all sorts of cargo including barrels of turpentine, bales of cotton, and bundles of lumber. In the meantime his son Willie had been born.

One day while Will was at work, several bales of cotton had fallen upon him and left him paralyzed and helpless. About a year later he had died and his funeral services had been held in a little Baptist church around the corner. Sadly his friends, who had packed the little church, had sung his favorite song, "I've Got a Home in-a Dat Rock . . . Don't You See?"

From then on Willie had lived with his mother, who had supported him until he had become old enough to work. After Willie had married Mayann, he had brought her to his mother's house to live. Nearby lived Josephine's mother, who had helped to look after Willie.

Now with the new baby Louis in the house, Willie was a proud father. His mother Josephine was a grandmother, and her mother was a great-grandmother, both of whom soon would play important parts in Louis' young life.

Great-Grand-mother Na-Na

THE LITTLE one-room house in James Alley was too small for three adults and a baby. Willie and his wife Mayann often argued and quarrelled. Finally one night when their son Louis was nearly a year old, Willie suddenly decided to leave. The next morning Mayann sadly put Louis in Mrs. Armstrong's arms and said, "Will you take care of him for a while, Grandma? I want to find work somewhere to earn money."

"I'm sorry you and Willie are having trouble," replied Mrs. Armstrong. "A man really needs a home of his own for raising a family."

Mayann picked up her chunky little son from

Grandma's lap and kissed him tenderly. Baby Louis smiled, but he didn't realize that it would be a long time before he would see his mother again. Soon she placed him gently back in Grandma's lap. Then she kissed Grandma on the forehead and walked out the door. She didn't look back because she knew that if she did, she wouldn't be able to leave.

Both Willie Armstrong and his wife Mayann found work. Willie obtained a job as a section boss in a turpentine factory in New Orleans. His wages were poor, but he regularly took a little money to Grandma Armstrong to help care for young Louis. In addition, Grandma did washing and ironing for white people in order to earn money. Several days a week she went to wash and iron at a white family's home. On those days her mother came to care for Louis.

Grandma Armstrong's mother was a small Creole woman with coffee-tan skin, thin features, and curly hair. She now was old, having been born a slave on a cotton plantation outside New Orleans. Louis was very fond of her and as a baby learned to call her Na-na.

Great-grandmother Na-na regularly entertained Louis by singing him religious songs called spirituals and telling him interesting stories. One day when she was caring for him she sat down in a rocker to get a pan of green beans ready to cook. She had just finished singing several spirituals as he had tapped the rhythm on a pan. "Now, Na-na," he said, "what story are you going to tell me today?"

"I don't know, Louis," she answered as she started to snap and stem the beans. "I've already told you all the stories I remember."

"Tell me the story again about the day you were freed," begged Louis.

Na-na stopped rocking and partially closed her eyes. She sighed solemnly and pressed her thin lips together. "I don't like to think about the horrible times when I was a slave," she explained. "Things are not good for Black people yet, but they certainly are much better than they were under slavery."

"How are they better?" asked Louis, not fully understanding.

Na-na put her beans aside and pulled Louis up from the floor. "Well, things are better for Black people today because they get paid money for working. Your grandmother gets paid money for doing washing and ironing. In slavery we didn't get any money for working. We had to work hard just to earn food and clothing and a little shack to live in."

Once more Na-na picked up her beans and Louis slid back down at her feet. "Now please tell me the story about being freed," he begged.

Na-na looked down and smiled. "Well, the big news came one Saturday afternoon when I

was twenty years old and Josephine was five," she began. "There was talk that something good had happened, but we couldn't figure out what it was. The overseer, or man who made us work, sent word that the Colonel, our master, wanted to see us. He ordered every man, woman, and child to gather in front of his big house early Sunday morning.

"The master was the man who owned us," Na-na continued. "He had bought my parents, and when I was born, he also owned me. Now since he owned all of us, if he ordered us to meet any place, we had to be there."

Louis interrupted. "That's one part of the story I don't like," he said.

Na-na went on. "The next morning we all gathered in front of the big house, dressed in our Sunday best."

"Sunday best?" asked Louis, looking up curiously. "What does that mean?"

26

"Well, it means the best clothes we had, the ones we wore to church," explained Na-na. "I wore a beautiful red dress with a white collar which the madam had given me."

"Was the madam the master's wife?" asked Louis, again interrupting the story.

"Yes," replied Na-na without further explanation. "As we stood on the lawn waiting, we started to sing gently. In front of us stood old Tom Ross. He was the plantation preacher. Also he was our leader.

"The Colonel stood on the front porch, dressed in a Prince Albert coat, black string tie, and white waistcoat. Close beside him at the right sat his wife in a rocking chair. At his left stood his two sons, who were just home from college. In the rear stood his two daughters with their husbands and children.

"Finally the Colonel began to speak. 'Good morning, dear friends,' he said solemnly. We were surprised by these words, because he owned us and didn't really think of us as friends. 'I have called all of you here this morning to bring you good news. For some time this slavery problem has bothered me. Now after today I hope to have peace within my soul.'

"As we listened to these solemn words, we wondered whether the Colonel was going to die. At once he continued, 'A while back Abraham Lincoln, President of the United States, signed a document called the Emancipation Proclamation or declaration of freedom. This proclamation declares that all men, women, and children in our country have a right to be free. My eldest son will read the proclamation to you.'

"The Colonel's eldest son stepped forward and read the proclamation. All the adults listened closely. I listened along with the others but really didn't know what the words meant.

"After the Colonel's son finished reading the

28

proclamation, the Colonel spoke again. 'Now that this proclamation has been issued, you may consider yourselves free,' he said. 'I have felt for a long time that you should be free to work and earn money for yourselves. In order to help you, I plan to give every man and woman among you fifteen dollars and every child five dollars. Also, I plan to give every family among you enough food to last a month.

" 'As free men and women, you are free to stay here or free to leave, just as you wish,' the Colonel continued. 'If you want to stay here, I'll hire you to work for pay. If you want to leave, I'll give you the money and rations which I have mentioned. Now take the rest of the day to decide what you want to do. Tomorrow morning, when the bell rings, be ready to let me know what you have decided.' "

"You decided to leave and come to New Orleans, didn't you?" asked Louis.

"Yes," replied Na-na. "I came here with my mother, my daughter Josephine, and all my brothers and sisters. My mother said it was important to be completely on our own."

Na-na now got up to put her pan of beans on the stove to cook. "Oh, no, Na-na, don't stop now," cried Louis, grabbing her skirt. "What did you do the rest of the day after the Colonel told you that you were free?"

Na-na smiled. "Well, we were so happy that we just celebrated. We shouted, jumped up and down, and cracked our heels together. We sang many songs such as 'Free at last, free at last! I thank God Almighty I'm free at last!' and 'Chillun, didn't God deliver Daniel? I told you God would answer prayer!'" Na-na stood up again. "Now I must get these beans on the stove before Josephine comes home."

"Yes, she'll soon be coming from work at the big house," said Louis. "I just wish that the people there would treat her better and not make her work so hard. Someday I'll take care of her so she won't have to work for them."

Na-na stopped and frowned. "Why, Louis, you mustn't dislike people you don't really know," she exclaimed. "Josephine has worked for this same family on the hill for years. Someday she must take you with her to work, so you can meet some of them."

Soon Na-na started to sing "Little David Play on Your Harp," and Louis picked up a spoon and began to beat the rhythm on a pan. At once the serious look on his face gave way to a broad smile. He was happy to be making music.

Lessons from Grandmother

GRANDMA Armstrong was a very busy woman. On weekdays she worked for white people in the community. On some days she went to the big house to work and on other days she did washings and ironings for people at her home. On Sunday she always spent all day at the little Baptist church around the corner.

Even though she was constantly busy, she took time to teach Louis many lessons. She was loving and kind when he was good but became stern when he disobeyed. Always she felt that he should be punished when he was wrong.

One of the first things that Grandma Armstrong tried to teach Louis was to keep himself clean. She explained to him that keeping clean was one of the most important things in life. Often she gave him a gentle shove toward the wash basin and said, "Soap and water will clean anything, even ears."

Louis knew what Grandma meant and would scrub his ears inside and out with soap and water. Then he would break out in a big grin and run to her for approval. Always she examined his ears carefully and rewarded him by patting him gently on the head.

Grandma not only taught Louis to keep his body clean, but she taught him to keep his clothes clean. She scrubbed and bleached and starched and ironed his clothes so that he could always take pride in wearing them. She wanted him to look clean and to feel clean.

As Louis became older, she taught him the value of money. When she had to deliver two baskets of laundry to people's homes, she paid him for carrying one of the baskets. "Helping me is your job," she said. "Every time you help me, I'll pay you a nickel."

The first day Grandma paid Louis, he felt very rich with a nickel in his pocket. "Can I spend it?" he asked as he pulled it out and held it tightly in his chunky little fist.

"Yes, you can spend it, but why?" she asked. "If you spend it you won't have it any more." Louis was too young to understand, but he could tell that she didn't want him to spend it.

Later that same day Grandma prepared to deliver two more baskets of laundry. She placed a freshly laundered apron over her dress so that she would look neat and clean. She put a bonnet over her thick black hair which was braided in a circle over each ear. "Now you can carry another basket for me," she said. "You must work if you expect to be paid."

Grandma started to open the door but thought of something more to say to Louis. "Don't spend all the money you have just because you have it. You must learn to save for a time when you may not get paid."

With these words she picked up one of the baskets and stepped outside. Louis picked up the other basket and started to follow her. Then suddenly he put down the basket and told her to wait while he went back into the house. In a few minutes he returned, picked up his basket again and said, "Now, Grandma, I'm ready."

"What was that all about?" she asked.

"I was saving for a time when I may not get paid," he answered with a grin. Grandma was very proud. Louis understood.

When Louis was four years old, Grandma moved into a larger house in the same section of New Orleans. This larger house had three rooms with a small yard in front and a larger yard at the back. Between this house and the next house there was an areaway so people could walk around to the back door.

The new house was of a shotgun type, because the rooms were located back of one another like the parts of a shotgun. In front there was a parlor or special room for entertaining friends. This room, which was the first room in the house, included all the best furniture. The next room behind the parlor was the bedroom, and the room at the back was the kitchen.

Most of Grandma's friends came to the back door. They liked to sit down in the kitchen and visit with her. In addition they liked the odor of good foods which always seemed to be cooking on the kitchen stove.

Louis liked this new house and yard, except for a Chinaball tree from which Grandma obtained switches for punishing him. One day she sent him to get a switch from the tree so she could whip him for not telling the truth. "What did he do?" asked Great-grandmother Na-na.

"Well, I sent him to the store and told him to hurry back," explained Grandma. "Then he stopped to play along the way and was an hour late getting home. When he came in, I scolded him and he said that he had been resting under the Chinaball tree in the back yard.

"Now I have to punish him," Grandma went on. "Once you taught me that a person who will lie will steal. Well, Louis has lied and I must teach him to tell the truth."

"You're right," said Great-grandmother Na-na, "but it will be hard to whip him."

Just then Louis came in with a switch, the smallest he could find on the tree. He handed it fearfully to his grandmother and waited to see what she would say. "Well, I see you have picked a very small switch," she said. "Now I'll have to whip you all the harder."

Louis knew that this time he had no escape from a whipping. Grandma grabbed him and started to whip him as hard as she could. Finally she stopped long enough to say in a commanding tone of voice, "A person who will lie will steal. You must not lie. Always tell the truth. Do you hear? Always tell the truth."

Then without giving him a chance to answer she grabbed him by the shoulders and shook him. "Never lie," she said. "Always tell the truth. Do you hear? Always tell the truth."

Louis never forgot this important lesson from Grandma. From that day on he never told a fib again. He always told the truth and expected other people to do the same.

On Sunday Grandma always took Louis to a little Baptist church a short distance from their home. She and Great-grandmother Na-na were leaders in the church. They went there in the morning on Sunday and stayed all day.

The children assembled about 10 o'clock for Sunday School, which included listening to Bible stories and singing. The chief storyteller was "Uncle" Henry, whose real name was Henry Jones. He was a tall, thin Zulu African who had been captured and sold into slavery. During the final days of slavery his master had taught him to read so that he could become a plantation preacher. Then on Sundays he had read the Bible and conducted services for other slaves. Sometimes the master had attended the Sunday morning meetings to listen to him.

After all the slaves had been freed, Uncle Henry had walked from one Black community to another to help with church services. Now he was living in New Orleans, where the church people gave him a place to stay. During the week he made a few dollars working at odd jobs.

At the little Baptist church he helped to conduct Sunday School for the children. Now and then he helped with the prayer meeting in the middle of the week. He could tell Bible stories well and make them come alive for both adults and children. Everybody liked him and his stories from the Bible.

Sometimes Uncle Henry opened the Sunday morning services by offering a prayer and leading the group in singing. One of his favorite songs was "When the Saints Go Marching In." This song also was a favorite with Louis. He sang happily along with the others and tapped the rhythm quietly on his knee.

The person who regularly led the singing in Sunday School was Miss Sarah. She understood children and knew how to choose songs that they enjoyed singing. Often Uncle Henry told the children an exciting story about dry bones in the valley that would rise again. Then Miss Sarah would have them sing a song that told how the bones finally got connected.

All the children were taught to be quiet in church and were punished severely for making noise. They understood that they were to be seen and not heard. Louis learned early that the church was God's house, where he must be reverent. He went in quietly and sat silently and listened, except during the singing. Then he sang loudly with the others.

The church had a benefit society to help members when they were in trouble. The members collected money for a special fund to help one another in cases of sickness or death. Uncle Henry kept a record of how much each person gave. Grandma Armstrong was in charge of the special fund and kept all the money. Nobody knew where she hid it, but she always brought whatever amount the benefit society decided to to give a family in trouble.

Louis learned many valuable lessons from going to church with Grandma Armstrong. First, he learned to respect the church as a house of worship and as a force for good in the community. Second, he learned many rules of behavior in getting along with others. Third, he learned from Grandma's benefit society the importance of saving money for times of trouble.

Louis' few years with Grandma Armstrong were both happy and helpful. He never forgot the important lessons that he learned from her. Among other things, she taught him to keep clean and neat and always to be honest.

With Grandma at the Big House

ONE MORNING Grandma Armstrong was getting ready to go to the big house to work. She surprised Louis by telling him that he could go with her. "You may play about the yard while I wash and iron," she said.

When they reached the house, Grandma knocked on the back door. The lady of the house came to the door. "How are you, Josie?" she asked with a smile. Then without waiting for an answer, she turned and called, "John, bring the dirty clothes for Josie to wash."

Soon a Black man brought two bundles of clothes to be washed. He greeted Grandma and carried the bundles to the back yard where she did most of her work. Louis stood and watched as she filled a tub with water and started to wash the dirty clothes.

Before long two little boys about four and five years of age came running toward Grandma. They lived in the big house on the hill and knew that she came there to work. When they saw Louis they stopped short in surprise. "Hello, Pierre and Henri," called Grandma. "I have brought my grandson Louis to play with you today."

When Louis saw the boys coming, he hid behind Grandma's long thick skirt. He peeped at them from behind her skirt and they strained their eyes trying to see him. "Come on out, Louis," she said as she reached down and gave him a shove. "Now you boys run and play while I go ahead with my work."

At first the two little boys stood and stared at

Louis, and he stood and stared at them. Finally Pierre, who was the older of the two boys, said to Louis hesitatingly. "Do you know how to play hide-and-seek?"

"Oh, yes," replied Louis with a grin. "I've played hide-and-seek many times with my friends at Grandma's home."

"Come on, then," said both of the boys, running toward a big tree.

Grandma stopped them for a moment to caution them to stay away from her washing. "I don't want you to crash into the tub so I'll have to scrub you, too," she said.

By now she had started to wash and moved her arms up and down swiftly in a tub full of clothes and sudsy water. Every now and then she paused to rub a garment vigorously to remove a stained spot. Then she rinsed it in clean water and examined it to make sure the spot was gone.

Grandma sang almost constantly to help keep

her mind busy as she worked. One of her favorites, which she sang often, went as follows:

"I've got a home in-a that rock, don't you
    see?
I've got a home in-a that rock, don't you
    see...don't you see?
I'm gonna lay down this load and stumble
    up-a that road.
There's a home up there in glory just for
    me . . . just for me."

"I'll be It to start the game," said Pierre when the boys reached the tree. "You, Louis, and you, Henri, may run and hide."

Pierre pretended to close his eyes on the trunk of the tree while Louis and Henri went to hide, but he slyly peeped to see where they were hiding. Louis found a hiding place back of a clump of bushes in the back yard and Henri hid behind a nearby tree.

As Louis waited, he laughed to himself because he thought he would be hard to find. Much to his surprise, however, Pierre came right to the spot and pulled back the bushes. Then he went to the nearby tree and found Henri.

"So soon?" asked Henri, puzzled.

"Yes, how could you find us so fast?" asked Louis, also puzzled.

Pierre only grinned. Then he said, "I have eyes in the back of my head. Just to prove it, I'll be It again."

Once more Pierre pretended to close his eyes on the trunk of the tree. Louis and Henri ran to hide, but this time Louis looked back briefly and caught Pierre peeping. "I see you peeping, Pierre," he called.

Again Pierre placed his face against the tree and pretended to close his eyes. Louis held back for a moment before he ran to hide and caught Pierre peeping again. "I see you, Pierre," he cried. "Once more you're peeping."

By now Pierre was so ashamed because Louis

had caught him cheating that he really closed his eyes. Louis tiptoed away and hid behind the same clump of bushes, and Henri tiptoed to join him. Pierre looked all round the yard, behind trees and buildings, but he never thought to look behind the clump of bushes again. Finally he had to give up looking.

Louis and Henri came out, happy to have stumped Pierre, but Pierre was angry and wanted to stop playing. He sauntered off by himself but came back about a half hour later. Then during the rest of the day the three boys had fun running about and playing tag. When Grandma and Louis started to go home, Louis said, "The next time I come, we'll play another game of hide-and-seek, and you won't be able to find me."

Pierre, still a little unhappy, said, "Oh, yes, I will. I'll study every place where you can hide and then I'll know where to look."

"Oh, no, you won't," replied Louis as he waved

good-by to the boys and went down the hill with his grandmother.

From then on Louis thought of possible places to hide when he played the next game with Pierre and Henri. Finally, one day Grandma said that he could go back to the big house with her. Since the day was exceptionally hot, she started to wash in the shade of a tree.

Pierre and Henri were happy to see Louis, and the three boys started to play right away. "I'll be It first," said Pierre, "because I want to show you that I can find you."

This was just what Louis had wanted, since he was eager to try out a new place to hide. This time Pierre didn't cheat because he thought he knew every possible place to look. Quietly and cautiously Louis crept under a pile of dirty clothes near where Grandma was busy washing. He curled up underneath the clothes to make sure none of his body could be seen.

Pierre soon found his brother Henri, but he couldn't find Louis. Before long Henri began to help Pierre look for Louis. They searched behind trees and bushes in the yard. They opened all the doors to the barn. Now and then Louis peeked out and saw them looking.

Grandma knew where Louis was hiding, but she kept on singing and scrubbing. When the boys came near, looking for him, she washed all the harder. Finally Louis became hot and tired under the pile of clothes. He stuck out his head from the clothes and said, "Boo!"

Pierre tagged him right away and said, "I found you. Now you're It."

Louis exclaimed, "No, sirree! I found myself. You wouldn't have found me if I hadn't stuck my head out. It was too hot for me to stay under the clothes any longer."

Pierre and Henri agreed that it was too hot to keep on playing. All three boys sat and rested in the shade of a tree.

Soon Grandma Armstrong finished washing and got ready to go home. As she and Louis headed down the hill, he waved good-by to the two brothers and they waved back. They had enjoyed this day of good, clean fun.

Off to a New Home

ONE EARLY fall day when Louis returned home from visiting his great-grandmother Na-na, he found an old woman in the front room talking with his grandmother. He noticed that she had a serious look on her face as if she were carrying on an important conversation. Somehow he was frightened because she looked at him curiously as he entered the room. He smiled, and she nodded, but she said nothing to him.

He walked over to his grandmother and stood beside her to listen. "Thank you for being such a good boy," she said, pulling him closer to her and giving him a big hug.

Louis thought that he could see tears in his grandmother's eyes and wondered what was troubling her. He wondered whether the old woman had brought her bad news of some kind. Finally she pulled him close to her again and said, "This lady lives near your mother Mayann. She has brought word that your mother is sick."

Louis looked over at the old lady and tried to remember his mother, but he couldn't. He hadn't seen either his mother or his father since he was a tiny baby. Sometimes his grandmother had told him about them, but he had been too young to remember them. Often he had wished that he could see them again.

His grandmother continued, "This lady says that you have a baby sister."

"A baby sister!" exclaimed Louis, once more looking over curiously at the old lady.

"Yes," replied Grandma, "and now that your mother is sick, she needs you. You will have to go live with her. I knew this would happen sooner or later, but I don't know what I'll do without you. Well, let me get your clothes."

Louis was stunned and waited quietly while his grandmother was gone. Soon she came back and handed him a bundle which contained all his clothes. "Here are two play outfits, one Sunday pair of pants, one Sunday shirt and a sleeping top," she said. "Now take good care of them when you get to your mother's."

Grandma's eyes filled with tears as she handed the bundle to Louis. "Stand up and let me straighten the collar of your shirt," she said. "I don't want Mayann to think that I haven't taken good care of you."

"Oh she won't," said Louis. "You have been very good to me, Grandma. I'll never forget how good you have been."

"Just remember all the things that I have taught you," said Grandma.

"I will," replied Louis. "I'll wash my face and hands and brush my teeth every day without being told."

"And don't forget to mind older folks and be kind to them," Grandma added.

"I'll remember, Grandma," said Louis, now ready to burst into tears.

Grandma patted him on the back and gently pushed him toward the door. He obediently followed the old lady along the street, but he kept looking back and waving. All the while his grandmother kept waving to him.

The old lady and Louis stopped at a corner to wait for a trolley car. Nearby there was a big prison called the House of Detention. Suddenly Louis put down his bundle of clothes and started to sob. The old lady grabbed him firmly by the shoulders and said sternly, "Stop that crying. Stop it right now."

Louis tried to stop crying, but his whole body

shook with sobs. Finally the old lady spoke again, this time in a threatening tone of voice. "If you don't stop crying at once, I'll have you put in that big prison."

This threat caused Louis to think of all the bad stories he had heard about the prison. At once he stopped crying and picked up his bundle of clothes. "Oh, please don't," he pleaded as he started to shake with fear. "Please don't put me in there."

Just then the trolley car came. It looked big like a house as it came down the middle of the street. There were two rows of seats in the car next to windows on both sides. Between the two rows of seats there was an aisle for walking. Persons could get on or off the trolley car by using either a front door or a side door in the middle of the car.

Louis had never ridden a trolley car, but he often had seen one. The old lady told him to

get on at the side door. He hopped on quickly and took a seat near the front of the car. Since the car was almost empty, he thought he could sit wherever he wanted to.

The old lady climbed on the car and found a seat in the rear. Then she looked about for Louis and found him sitting near the front. She waved for him to come back with her, but by now he was too busy looking at sights out of the window to notice her.

Finally she jumped up and rushed up front where he was sitting. She grabbed him by the collar and shouted, "Come on back here, boy, where you belong." She led him to the back of the car, pointed to a sign, and said, "This sign says we're supposed to sit back here."

Louis' eyes opened wide. He couldn't understand why he had to move, because there were empty seats everywhere in the car. Finally he asked, "What does the sign say?"

"It says 'FOR COLORED PASSENGERS ONLY.' That means we sit back here and white folks sit up there." She went to a seat, sat down with a plop, and pulled Louis down beside her. Louis opened his mouth to speak, but she frowned and said, "Don't say anything. Just sit. We're going to get off soon."

The ride had been spoiled for Louis, and he sat staring straight ahead. Suddenly the old lady nudged him and said gruffly, "Come on. It's time to get off."

Two blocks from the trolley line, they reached his mother's little house. When they entered the door, Louis found his sick mother lying in bed. His little sister toddled up to him, holding out her hand. He held out his hand for hers.

"Where's my father?" he asked the old lady quietly. "Is he at work?"

"He's at work, but he doesn't come home," replied the old lady. "He's gone and you can see that your mother needs you. I have to leave for home now to fix my husband's supper. Take care of your mother and sister." She turned to speak to Louis' sick mother before she left. "I have to go now, Mayann," she said.

"Thank you," Mayann told her, smiling weakly as she spoke. In a second the old lady left, closing the door softly behind her.

Louis immediately walked over to his mother's bed and bent over to kiss her. "I'm so glad you could come, son," she said. "I need you now, but I'll soon be up and about."

All the while Louis's little sister kept tugging at his arm. He felt big beside her. "What's her name?" he asked.

"Beatrice," replied his mother almost in a whisper, "but your father always called her 'Mama Lucy,' and that name stuck."

Louis held his sister's hand tightly. He felt like a man, but he was only a little boy.

Reunion with Mother Mayann

LOUIS' mother lived in a single room on a back courtyard. There was no yard or open space about the house where the children could play. All the sleeping, cooking, washing, ironing, and entertaining had to be done in this one room. Even so, the room was clean and comfortable.

At first, as Louis looked about the crowded room, he wondered where he would sleep. He missed his grandmother and her larger house and yard, but he knew that he would be happy here. He loved his mother and realized that she needed him, and he already loved his little sister, Mama Lucy. She still held to his hand.

Louis noticed that his mother looked weak and frail as she lay quietly under the spotless bed clothes. "I was afraid your grandmother wouldn't let you come, since I hadn't come to see you," she said. "Life has been hard with me. Your father and I have had many arguments. After our last argument, he said that he wouldn't be back. I was wrong in some of the things I said and can't blame him for leaving."

"How old is Mama Lucy?" asked Louis, trying to change the subject.

"She is just two years old and smart for her age," replied Mayann. She smiled at both children standing by the bed, hand in hand. "You are smart, too, for your age. Always remember that your health is the best thing to have. When you are sick, you can't work and nobody has time for you. Most of my friends work except a few, including the old lady who came after you. Your father paid her to come."

Mayann shifted her position on the two pillows under her head and looked directly at Louis. "It's good to have money, but nothing takes the place of good health," she said. "Promise me that you will always take care of your health." She waited for his answer.

"I promise," said Louis, not really knowing what he was promising.

"Good," said Mayann. "Now let me show you one way to care for your health. Get a chair and look for a box of pills in the top drawer of my dresser." She pointed to the top drawer. Louis got the chair, climbed up and looked about in the drawer. Soon he found a small box of pills under some garments. He hopped down and took the box to his mother.

Mayann reached out for the box of pills. "These are 'Coal Roller' pills, Louis," she said, opening the box and taking out a few little black pills for him to see.

"Your body is just like a machine," she continued. "It has to be cleaned out to keep it working well. If you take these little pills regularly they will drive all the sick germs out of your body. Do you understand how important all this is for you?" She raised up a little to make her point clear.

"I understand," said Louis as he eyed the little black pills.

"Now take three of the pills with a glass of water," she instructed. "You'll find some water over there in the bucket by the back door."

Obediently Louis got a glass of water and came back to the bed where his mother could see him. She watched him put the pills in his mouth and swallow them with the water. Then he waited to see what she would say.

"That's a good boy," said Mayann, smiling. She sank back on the pillows. Louis stood glued to the spot, not sure what would happen next.

Mama Lucy slipped her pudgy little hand into his and waited with him beside the bed. Soon Mayann sat up and said, "Now, son, get fifty cents which you'll find hidden under the carpet. Take this money and go to Rampart Street. That is the first busy street where there are stores and shops. Go to the store called Zattermann. Repeat the name, Zattermann."

Louis repeated the name, "Zattermann."

Mayann continued, "Get a slice of meat, a pound of red beans, and a pound of rice at the store. Repeat what you are to get."

Louis repeated the three items in the same order as Mayann had given them.

"Next go to the bakery next door and get two loaves of bread," said Mayann. "Then hurry home. Now, repeat all the instructions."

Louis repeated the instructions. Mayann smiled as she noticed how well he remembered everything. Louis was happy with himself.

He told Mama Lucy, "I can't take you because I have to do man's work." Gently he took his hand from hers and started proudly for the door.

"Be careful, son," cautioned his mother.

"I will," he assured her. He seldom had gone places alone before. His grandmother usually had taken him wherever he went. She had told him that he had to show that he could be trusted before he could go places alone. Now he had a chance to prove he was old enough to run an errand and to follow directions.

When he came around to the front of the house, he found six dirty, ragged boys standing on the sidewalk. He spoke to them and started to go on his way, but they stopped him. They blocked his path and crowded around him. One boy seemed the leader of the group. He was the dirtiest of all of them, and had a patch on one of his eyes.

"Are you a mama's boy?" he asked with a sneer.

"What's that?" Louis asked, as he tried to

move on. The group still blocked his path. Louis was surprised because he thought that even tough boys had some manners.

He had known a boy from his old neighborhood who wore a patch on one of his eyes. He had fallen on a dead tree and one of the twigs had punched his eye out. Louis remembered that all the neighborhood was sad because no one had the money for a doctor, so a patch was put on the boy's eye. Louis tried to feel sorry for this boy with the patch on his eye, but he couldn't.

There had been tough boys back in his grandmother's neighborhood, but they had been taught to leave people alone and to treat people with respect. He had thought that all tough boys were alike, but he was realizing very fast that these boys were different.

The boy with the patch was the biggest boy and the leader of the gang of boys. Louis learned later that they called him One-eye Bud. The patch made him look tougher than he really was.

One-eye Bud moved closer and grabbed Louis by the collar of his suit. His dirty hand made a smudge where it touched the collar. This wasn't Louis' best suit, but it was clean and neat. He wasn't wearing any shoes.

One-eye Bud looked into Louis' face and jeered, "So you don't know what we're talking about? Well, since you're new around here, we have to let you know who's boss of this alley." Then suddenly he grabbed up a handful of mud and smeared it over the front of Louis' suit. All the other boys in the gang laughed.

Louis was bewildered, and though he felt a twinge of pity as he looked at the dirty boys, he knew he had to do something to prove that he wasn't afraid of them. He also knew that he couldn't whip all of them at once.

All at once Louis whirled and socked Bud with

a smashing blow in the face. He hit Bud's mouth so hard that it began to bleed. Then all the boys scampered away, with Bud following them.

Louis hurried to the store and bakery and started home carrying two large bags. As he hurried along, he stepped on a big rusty nail sticking up from a board. He felt pain but hurried on, eager to reach home.

When he entered the door, he was surprised to find his mother sitting up in bed, looking much better. She smiled as he put the two bags down on the table. "Did you have any trouble?" she asked, noticing how dirty he was.

"No trouble except that I stepped on a nail," said Louis, pointing to his foot.

"Oh, my!" cried Mayann. "We must do something about it at once. Limp next door and get my friend, Miss Sally Lee."

Soon Louis came back with Miss Sally Lee. "This is my son," explained Mayann. "He has stepped on a nail. Please wash his foot while I prepare a couple of mixtures of herbs and roots. You'll find hot water on the stove."

Miss Sally filled a pan with hot water, but when Louis put his foot in the water, he jerked his foot out and cried, "Ouch!"

"Put your foot back in there," ordered Miss Sally. "You'll just have to stand it." She held his knee to keep his foot in the water.

In a few minutes Mayann went to one of the pots she had simmering on the stove. She took a wad of gummy mixture from the pot and put it on the nail hole in Louis' foot. Then she wrapped his foot tightly with a clean rag. Next she took some of the mixture from the other pot and put it aside to cool. "Now put on your night clothes and get into bed," she said, pointing to the one bed in the room. "Climb in on the other side of the bed."

"Let me help him, Mayann," offered Miss Sally. "You must be all tuckered out."

"Yes, I am," replied Mayann, "but when a child is hurt, a mother just seems to pick up energy from someplace to look after him."

Louis looked down at his bundle of clothes, still unopened in a corner of the room. "Oh, I'm sorry," said Mayann. "I forgot all about your clothes. Let me get out a top for you." She opened the bundle and handed a top to Louis. Then she opened a dresser drawer and put his other clothes away neatly. All were clean and freshly ironed.

"What else can I do?" asked Miss Sally, anxious to keep on helping.

"Give Louis a cup of that pluto water I have cooling on the stove," said Mayann, dropping wearily in a chair.

"Is that what you call this liquid?" asked Miss Sally as she took a cupful to Louis, now in bed. Mayann nodded, meaning "Yes."

Louis tasted the liquid, made a face, and held the cup away from his mouth. "Drink it, son," ordered Mayann. "It may taste nasty, but it will burn the poison out of you."

Louis tried again and finally got the stuff down. Miss Sally took the glass and adjusted the bed covers over his body. Mayann placed a cool wet cloth on his forehead. "Now try to get some sleep," she said softly.

Louis closed his eyes and soon was fast asleep. Mama Lucy stood beside the bed and watched him closely. "Brudder sleep?" she asked.

"Let me get some supper for her before I go," said Miss Sally.

"Thank you, Miss Sally," said Mayann. "She probably is very hungry. Also I hope you can wash her and put her to bed for me."

"Don't worry," said Miss Sally. "I'll take care of her. Now you go to bed and rest."

Mayann crept into her side of the bed. She looked over proudly at Louis, who was lightly snoring. "Did I tell you he will start to school as soon as his foot is better? He is big for his age, isn't he, Miss Sally?"

"He really is," agreed Miss Sally.

"And smart, too," added Mayann as she sank back on her pillow with a smile on her face.

Schoolboy and Paper Boy

AFTER THE PAIN left Louis' foot, Mayann took him to the nearby Fisk School. She was proud to have the neighbors see her taking him to school. When they reached the building, they found the principal, Arthur P. Williams, at the front door, watching children stream up the steps. He greeted Mayann and Louis and took them to his office. Then he returned to the door to continue watching the children.

Mr. Williams smiled as he stood at the door and greeted the children, many of them by name. He had a reputation for being strict, but the children liked him and thought he was fair.

When they violated rules or got out of hand, he nearly always whipped them. In addition, he gave them long lectures on how they were supposed to behave. The children did not want to be sent to him for punishment, because they felt it was a big disgrace.

After all the children had arrived, Mr. Williams returned to his office. "Now I'm ready to talk with you," he said pleasantly.

"Well, I'm Mayann Armstrong and this is my son Louis," explained Mayann. "He has been living with his grandmother in another part of the city, but now he is living with me."

"Hello, Louis," said Mr. Williams, holding out his hand. "We're happy to have you."

"I'm sorry to bring him late," said Mayann, "but last week he stepped on a nail and injured his foot." She pointed to Louis' foot, which was still bandaged tightly. Louis held his foot so the principal could see it.

76

Mr. Williams picked up a big record book from his desk and wrote down Louis' name. "Where is the boy's father?" he asked.

Mayann dropped her eyes. "His father and I always have had problems," she replied, "and he has left me several times. Not long ago we had a terrible argument, and he left me again. This time he declared that he never would come back, and I don't think he will." She paused for a moment, raised her head proudly, and continued. "But we'll get along. I'll work to earn money. Louis will be here every day."

Mr. Williams stopped her. "You need not be ashamed," he said sympathetically. "We have many children whose fathers no longer live at home. Our menfolks become frustrated and helpless when they can't earn enough money to provide decent homes for their families. Most of them have little schooling, if any, and don't know how to look for better jobs.

"When people live in crowded homes, they often quarrel," Mr. Williams continued. "One word leads to another, and they say things they don't mean to say. Then they separate and the children often suffer."

Mayann dropped her head, and again Mr. Williams stopped talking. "You're right," she said solemnly. "I was sick when my husband and I last quarreled, and I said terrible things to him. I don't know why, but I did. If I had been in his place, I would have left, too. He won't be back, but he still pays my rent. I know, because when I went to pay it the other day, I found that somebody had already paid it."

"I didn't mean to pry into your private affairs," said Mr. Williams. "I just wanted you to know how important it is to keep Louis in school. If he learns all he can while he is young, he'll be able to get a better job than his father. He'll be able to provide better for himself and whatever family he may have. Then he will be happier and his family will be happier."

"I will do my best to keep him in school, Mr. Williams," promised Mayann.

"Now let me tell you a few things about the Fisk School," said Mr Williams. "It starts with grade one and extends to the sixth grade. The children come here from many sections of the city. All our teachers are women, and we expect the children to obey them. The teachers' names are Rose Fleming, Madeline M. Campanel, Aurora V. Peters, Annie Lehman, Deborah B. Johnson, Ellen E. Colwell, Mary A. McDowell, Fannie C. Williams, Maria M. Wicker, and Emily Barney. You may know some of them."

"Yes, two of them go to our church," replied Mayann proudly.

"We have a woman janitor," added Mr. Williams, "and the children must cooperate with her to keep the building and yard clean. They must not track mud into the building when they come in from playing outside. They must not litter up the floors and grounds with trash and left-over food. There are special barrels where they may throw things away.

"The vice-principal is Miss Victoria Pearson. She is my assistant and helps me to run the school. The children must be courteous to her and obey all her orders.

"All our children are supposed to come to school clean and on time every morning. We believe that cleanliness and punctuality are very important. We stress learning to read, spell, write, and figure in our classrooms. We teach a little singing but no instrumental music. At present, we have no musical instruments, but we hope to get some before long.

"At recess, the children are free to play and have fun. They must play on the schoolgrounds except when it rains. Then they must play in an open place under the building. When recess is over, Miss Pearson rings a bell to call them back to their classrooms."

As Mr. Williams spoke, Louis realized that he would be very strict and that all the teachers would be strict. At the same time he could tell that Mr. Williams was interested in his pupils. He wouldn't be afraid to talk with him, if he had some kind of problem.

Finally Mr. Williams stopped talking and Mayann thanked him for being so helpful. Then as she started to leave, she turned to Louis and said, "Do you think you can find your way home all by yourself, son?"

Before Louis could answer, Mr. Williams said, "Don't worry any more about him. I'll find an older boy to see that he gets home safely after school. I don't want him to run into a gang of bad boys along the way. They might try to bully him or pick a fight with him."

Louis started to say that he already had run into a gang of boys but decided to keep still. Nobody had asked him about the trouble he had had, so there was no need to talk.

After Mayann left, Mr. Williams took Louis to his room. He introduced him to his teacher and said, "Be a good boy here, Louis. If you have any problems, come to see me."

That afternoon Mr. Williams brought a big boy to show Louis the way home. When Louis entered the house, his mother made him rest his foot, which hurt a little from walking. Then she prepared him a good supper and made him go to bed extra early for the night.

At the end of the week, when Louis went out to play, he found One-eye Bud and his gang looking for him. "We've been hunting for you all week," said One-eye Bud. "Where in the world have you been? Going to school?"

"Yeah, all week," replied Louis.

"Do you like school?" asked another boy in the gang curiously.

"Yes, I really do," answered Louis. "Don't any of you guys go to school?"

"Naw," bragged One-eye Bud. "School folks don't miss us and we don't miss them."

Louis was puzzled by this attitude. "What do you do all day?" he asked.

"Oh, lots of things," replied One-eye Bud. "We hang around the streets and pick up a few pennies by stealing or working a little."

"Well, if you would go to school, you could learn to read, spell, write, and figure," explained Louis. "Then when you grow up, you could get a good job." He felt important trying to tell One-eye Bud what he was missing.

"I don't believe it," argued One-eye Bud. "No Black persons around New Orleans can get good jobs. Some can't even get anything to do." He was convinced that he was right.

"Can any of them read?" asked Louis.

"Of course not," replied One-eye Bud impatiently. "I don't know of any Black persons around here who can read."

"Well, I do," replied Louis. "All the teachers at school and all the leaders at church can read. My mother says that the teachers make thirty dollars a month. That's a lot of money just for being able to read."

For a moment One-eye Bud was silenced. "Yes, that's a lot of money," he agreed.

"Then why don't you go to school so you can get a good job later?" asked Louis.

One-eye Bud hesitated. "I'm not ready yet," he said, eager to change the subject. "Would you like to play army with us?"

"How do you play it?" asked Louis.

"We march along the street and pretend we're soldiers," explained One-eye Bud. "I'm the general of our army and you can be a sergeant."

"What does a sergeant do?" asked Louis.

"Well, when a soldier gets hurt, the sergeant rescues him and leads him to a safe place," replied One-eye Bud.

"That sounds important," said Louis. "I'll try being a sergeant in your army." He smiled and all the members of the gang smiled.

From then on Louis spent many hours playing army with the gang. One day when he was pretending to lead a soldier to safety, a board fell off a roof and hit him on the head. He dropped to the ground unconscious. Then One-eye Bud and a couple of others carried him home and placed him on the bed. "What happened to him?" cried his mother frantically.

"A board fell off a roof and hit him on the head," replied One-eye Bud. "I'm One-eye Bud and Dipper is my friend."

"Dipper?" asked Mayann in surprise. "Why do you call him Dipper?"

One-eye Bud hesitated. "Well, we call him Dipper because he has a large mouth like a dipper. You don't mind, do you?"

"Oh, no," replied Mayann. "Please run next door and tell Miss Sally Lee to come here at once to help me look after Louis."

In the meantime Mama Lucy went to the bed and began to stroke one of Louis' limp arms. Louis opened his eyes, and she called, "Oh, look, Brudder wake up."

"What's wrong with him?" asked Miss Sally as she rushed in and saw Louis in bed.

"A board fell on his head and knocked him out," explained Mayann, starting to rub his head with a clean damp cloth. She and Miss Sally applied a mixture of roots and herbs to his head. They gave him a large glass of pluto water to drink. Then they allowed him to go to sleep.

The next morning Louis was all right again. He surprised the gang by coming out to play.

"You're tough, Dipper, real tough," said One-eye Bud with admiration.

During the coming weeks and months Louis became deeply interested in school and had less time for playing. Most of all he became interested in learning to read. Every afternoon he brought something home to read to Mama Lucy.

Mayann spent most of her time cleaning, washing, ironing, and cooking in people's homes. Sometimes she worked in nearby restaurants and hotels. In the evenings when she came home, she sat down in a comfortable chair to rest. Then Louis would sit nearby on the floor and read to her. Reading to his mother made him feel grownup, like the man of the house.

Before long, he could read almost anything in print, even newspapers and magazines. Often Mayann brought home old newspapers or magazines for him to read. Now and then he read important articles to older folks in the neighborhood. Everybody was amazed by how he could read for a boy of his age.

When Mayann or her friends worked at restaurants or hotels, she often brought home leftover food, such as steaks, chops, and chickens. With this extra food she prepared especially good lunches for Louis to take to school. He not only had enough food for himself, but enough extra to share with some of his friends.

One-eye Bud and his gang learned about Louis' good lunches. Suddenly one noon they appeared at school and called, "What do you have good to eat today?"

"Come and see," Louis called back. At once the boys barged in like a swam of bees and ate as if they were starved.

Louis enjoyed seeing them, even though they were only street urchins. They knew the tough ways of the street, but they were proud to have him as a friend. They remembered their first meeting with him and still thought he was tough. Louis often chuckled about that meeting.

When Louis was seven years old, he started to sell newspapers, and within a couple of years he worked up a good newspaper business. Each day he filled his wagon with newspapers to deliver to people's homes. In addition, he stood on street corners and sold papers to people passing by. "Daily paper! Get your paper! Get your paper here!" he shouted.

All of Louis' customers liked him. Often a customer would call to him, "Hello, Dipper, I want a paper." Then when the customer would pay him, Louis would say, "Thank you," bow slightly, and break into a broad grin.

Louis regularly took money home to his mother and sister. Also he remembered what his grandmother had taught him about saving some of his money. He put a little money away for a time when he might not have a job.

Sometimes One-eye Bud and his gang hung around while Louis was handling his newspapers. Louis felt sorry for them, as he noticed how ragged and dirty they looked. He knew they were hungry and wondered whether they even had homes. Finally one day he asked One-eye Bud whether he would like to have a job.

"Naw," replied One-eye Bud. "Why should I have a job now? I'll wait till I grow up."

"Then it may be too late," cautioned Louis. "By starting to work now you can get a better job later. If you're willing to help me with my papers, you can start to earn now."

"What would I have to do?" asked One-eye Bud.

"Just fold the papers like this," replied Louis. He really didn't need to have the papers folded but merely wanted to help One-eye Bud earn a few nickels, if he could. One-eye Bud took the job but kept it only a short time.

At Church with Mother Mayann

ACROSS THE street from Mayann's home there was a church. This church was a large frame building, which had been built by the men in the congregation. At one end inside there was an elevated platform for the preacher and choir. The preacher at the church was Elder Cozy, noted for his fiery sermons. People came from all over the city to hear him preach.

One year Elder Cozy decided to hold a week of revival meetings. There would be religious services at the church every night for a week to help people revive their faith in God. There would be preaching, praying and singing.

Mayann hadn't attended church regularly, but she decided to take Louis and Mama Lucy to the first night of the revival meetings. All of them dressed in their best clothes and went to the church early. Soon the benches in the church were filled with people.

The services started with choir singing an opening song, entitled "Somebody's Knockin' at Your Door." At first the choir sang the words of the song softly, as follows:

"Somebody's knockin' at your door,
Somebody's knockin' at your door,
O, sinner, why don't you answer?
Somebody's knockin' at your door.
  Knock like Jesus,
  Knock like Jesus.
O, sinner, why don't you answer?
Somebody's knockin' at your door."

The choir repeated the song several times, each time singing the words somewhat faster and more loudly. All the people joined in the singing and rocked and swayed to the rhythm. Louis couldn't understand what was happening, but he sang and swayed with the others. He liked the music and all the excitement.

Before long Louis was surprised by the actions of his mother. As the singing continued, she closed her eyes and called out, "Yes, Lord. Yes, yes, Lord." She seemed to be overcome by the words and the music.

Finally everybody stopped singing, and Elder Cozy went to the pulpit to preach. He chose the following words for his subject, "Behold, I stand at the door and knock. If any man hear my voice, and open the door, I will come in to him." Mayann and all the others bent forward to catch every word Elder Cozy said.

"My friends," said Elder Cozy in an appealing voice, "did someone come knocking at your door? Did you let Him in?" He repeated the

94

question time and time again, and Mayann kept saying, "Yes, Lord. Yes, yes, Lord."

Next Elder Cozy built up the idea of the Lord knocking at each person's heart. He tried to make everybody feel aroused about getting religion. Finally he closed by repeating the words, "Did you let Him in? Did you let Him in, my friends, or did you pretend you didn't hear Him? What did you do when He knocked? What did you do? What did *you* do?"

When Elder Cozy finished preaching his sermon people all over the church, including Mayann, were excited. In a pleading voice he called for persons who did not belong to the church to come down front to the mourner's bench. "Will you come? Will you come?" he pleaded, extending his arms in an inviting manner. Again people started to sing and many started to the mourner's bench. Louis watched, overcome with curiosity about what was happening.

Suddenly Mayann started to shriek and sway back and forth. She threw up her arms wildly and accidentally knocked Louis off his seat. Then she started to jump up and down and he had to crawl under a bench for protection. Soon several church members came to quiet her, but had a hard time. Finally they succeeded and led her down to the mourner's bench.

As Louis watched the church members trying to calm his mother, he became amused and started to laugh. He didn't understand what was going on, but he thought everything was funny. The longer he watched, the more amused he became. Later, when he watched his mother and others join the church, he decided that things hadn't been funny after all.

After the church services were over, Mayann came to join Louis and Mama Lucy, who were waiting at the front door. She shook hands with Elder Cozy and said, "These are my two

children Louis and Mama Lucy. They will be coming to Sunday School regularly."

"Very good, my young friends," he said pleasantly. "I'll see you on next Sunday."

When Mayann and the children reached home, she tore into Louis and whipped him severely without a word of explanation. Then she fell exhausted into a nearby chair and started to cry. Neither Louis nor Mama Lucy could figure out what the whipping was for. Finally Mama Lucy asked, "What's wrong, Mama?"

At once Mayann stopped crying. Angrily she turned to Louis and said, "You should be ashamed of what you did at church tonight."

"What did I do?" asked Louis, bewildered.

"What did you do?" repeated Mayann. "Surely you know without asking. You laughed at me when I was getting converted."

"Converted? What's that?" asked Louis.

"Changing my way of life," Mayann answered. "I'm sorry, son," she continued apologetically. "I should have taken you to church just as your Grandma Armstrong did, but on Sunday mornings I always was too tired to get up early. Now that I've been converted, I'm going to go to church and lead a different life."

Louis remained quiet because he could tell that his mother had more to say. "After the revival meetings are over, I'll be baptized in the Mississippi River along with many others. That's the final step of being converted. From then on I'll be a member of the church."

"What do you mean by saying you'll be baptized?" asked Louis.

"I mean that I'll have my sins washed away," replied Mayann. "Your Grandma Armstrong had you baptized when you were a baby, but you were too young to remember."

"She did!" exclaimed Louis in great surprise. "Then do I have religion?"

"Yes, in a way," replied Mayann, "but when you get older you may want to get religion on your own. People have babies baptized so the babies will go to heaven if they die before they are old enough to know right from wrong. That's why Grandma Armstrong had you baptized."

Louis didn't understand all his mother was telling him, but he felt pleased to know he had been baptized. Finally he interrupted to ask her another question. "What does being converted do to people?"

"Being converted makes people want to lead better lives and avoid getting into trouble," explained Mayann. "They try to do the best they can with what they have and don't worry about what other people have. Now that I have been converted, you'll see a big change in me. I'll be a better mother to you."

Mayann, Louis, and Mama Lucy went to the revival meetings all the rest of the week. Louis now understood the meetings better and began to enjoy them. Most of all, he enjoyed the music. He learned to sing all the songs and to beat the rhythm on his knee.

After Elder Cozy's revival meetings ended, he baptized fifty-two people in the Mississippi River. Louis and Mama Lucy watched closely as he dipped their mother into the water. They were happy when this last step in her being converted was over. From then on she found more time to be with them, and the three of them spent many happy hours together.

The church was a very busy place. Mayann and the children attended the regular services and many special services which were held there. Louis never forgot the first funeral service he attended at the church. Sally Lee's husband, whose name was John, had become seriously ill and died. All his friends chipped in and hired a brass band to play at the funeral.

The night before the funeral, the neighbors held a wake at Sally Lee's home. They brought food and stayed all night with her and her family. From time to time they sang hymns and read verses from the Bible. Louis enjoyed taking part in the singing, but finally fell asleep in a corner of the room.

The next day relatives and friends gathered at Elder Cozy's church to attend Mr. John's funeral services. They came from all parts of the city, Uptown, Downtown, Front o' Town and Back o' Town, to pay their last respects to a man whom they had loved. Outside the church the Onward Brass Band waited to lead the funeral procession to the cemetery. This was one of the leading brass bands in the city.

During the funeral services Louis and his mother sat with Sally Lee and her family. Once his mother had told him of a funeral where the body had sat up and frightened everyone out of the church except Elder Cozy. Now he kept watching the casket closely, wondering whether Mr. John would sit up.

Finally the choir and congregation sang "Nearer My God to Thee." While they were singing, Elder Cozy walked slowly to the door, followed by pallbearers carrying the casket. Next came the members of the family with Louis and his mother. Louis was relieved that Mr. John hadn't sat up during the services.

Outside the church the Onward Brass Band started to play softly, with Joe "King" Oliver and Emmanual Perez playing cornets, Eddie Jackson playing the bass tuba, Black Benny the bass drum, and Babe Mathews the snare drum. Relatives and friends followed the band from the church to the cemetery, crying as they slowly trudged along behind. Louis cried along with the others, but he wasn't sure why.

The band continued to play while the body

was lowered into the grave. Black Benny beat the bass drum lightly to soften its tone and Babe Mathews put a handkerchief over his snare drum to give it a soft "Tom-tom" beat. Elder Cozy completed the ceremony by offering a prayer.

There was a brief pause, after which the atmosphere completely changed. The band struck up the hymn, "When the Saints Go Marching In," and marched off toward town with the crowd following. Louis watched everything the band did. He especially watched Joe "King" Oliver, the leader of the band. He didn't really know Oliver's name, but he liked his music.

As Louis marched along gaily with the crowd, he beat out the rhythm with his hands. He was caught up with the spirit that followed the funeral, the first he had ever attended.

From Streets to Waifs' Home

IN TIME, Mayann and her two children moved to a two-room house in a nearby section of the city called Brick Row. A short distance away there was a dance hall. Often on Saturday nights, Louis and some of his friends sneaked down to the hall to listen to the music.

First the band played in front of the dance hall to attract a crowd. Then it moved inside and the people followed to begin dancing. Later in the evening couples took turns doing special dances, each couple trying to outdo the others. Louis and his friends peeped through the cracks in the walls of the building to watch these special dances. Sometimes they tried to imitate the dances.

The streets in this section of the city were filled with music. The waffle man played a bugle to get people to buy his waffles. The pie man played a triangle to let people know he was near. The banana man man sang, "Yellow, ripe bananas, only fifteen cents a bunch."

Louis enjoyed all this music on the streets and obtained jobs singing with the junk man and the coal man. From these two jobs he regularly brought home small sums of money to his mother and sister. When he was with the junk man, he sang out, "Old rags and bones, folks! Old rags and bones!" The rich folks brought out all kinds of good clothes which he and the junk man sold cheaply to the poor.

When Louis was with the coal man, he cried, "Coal for your stoves, folks, a nickel a bucket! Coal for your stoves, a nickel a bucket!"

Often, when he was working on the coal cart, he stopped at a dance hall to listen to a popular pianist, named Jelly Roll Morton. Louis was greatly interested in this pianist because he had a gold-plated front tooth with a diamond setting. As he played, he continuously smiled to display the diamond in his tooth.

When Louis was twelve, he and three boys, known as Little Mac, Big Nose Sidney, and Georgie Greg, organized a quartet. All of them wore long pants to make them look older. Louis sang tenor because his voice still hadn't changed. He played a little slide whistle which operated somewhat like a trombone.

The boys chose "My Brazilian Beauty" as their theme song. No one had any idea where Brazil was or whether there really was such a place. Often they sang in places where minors weren't allowed to enter. After they sang, they passed a hat and received generous sums of money.

Many night Louis took a dollar home to his mother. He was happy to be able to help her pay the family expenses.

Mayann had noticed how grown-up Louis was getting, and decided it was time they had a talk. She explained that he was the "man of the house." Louis felt very proud. But his mother also told him that even though he was so grown-up now, he was never to go in the second drawer of her chest.

"You don't need anything in that drawer," she said. "Someday, I will show you what's in there. But for now, you are to stay away."

Of course, Louis became curious about the drawer and decided to take a peek. He went to the chest and opened the drawer. He carefully looked through the papers. Buried under all the papers was a gun. As Louis looked at it, he felt very guilty. He quickly covered it back up and shut the drawer.

On New Year's Eve, December 31, 1913,

Louis remembered the gun. He knew people would be shooting off guns to celebrate the new year. People liked to shoot guns off into the air. They didn't think anybody could get hurt. Louis decided he wanted to shoot his gun. So he put it in his pocket and ran off to meet his friends.

Louis and Little Mac, Big Nose Sidney, and Georgie Greg met on the street corner. They were planning to sing up and down the street.

But first Louis showed them his mother's gun; they were eager for him to use it. Louis didn't want to right then, so he put it back in his pocket. The four boys started their singing. They noticed One-eye Bud's group across the street. They were also singing.

Suddenly One-eye Bud pulled out a small gun and shot three times in the air. "Now it's your turn, Dipper," said Louis' friends.

Louis hesitated. He knew he was wrong for several reasons. He was wrong to have betrayed his mother's trust in him. He was wrong to have brought the gun someplace he could hurt someone with it. Louis thought about what he was doing and felt very guilty. But his friends egged him on. He couldn't back down.

"Come on, Dipper. That little noise they made with their play pistol is nothing to what you can do with a real gun. Come on. You show them!" Big Nose Sidney said.

Louis pulled out the pistol and shot several times in the air. *Boom! Boom! Boom!* sounded the pistol. One-eye Bud and his gang looked across the street in amazement. Louis' friends, frightened by the noise, fled to hide in the crowd.

A tall policeman appeared out of nowhere. He grabbed Louis by the arm and seized the pistol. Louis looked around for all his friends. They had all left him alone to face the music of his wrong actions.

"What do you mean, shooting a pistol here in the street?" The policeman asked gruffly.

"Oh, please, Mister Policeman, I didn't mean to do any harm," pleaded Louis.

The policeman ignored Louis and put him in jail. The next morning, Louis still was frightened. He wondered how serious a crime he had committed and what punishment he would receive. He wished that somehow he could talk with his mother, but she didn't even know where he was.

While Louis sat thinking, a man came to the cell carrying a bunch of keys. "Are you Louis Armstrong?" he asked.

"Yes, sir," replied Louis.

"Then come with me," said the man, unlocking the cell door. "We're going to take you to the Colored Waifs' Home for Boys."

Outdoors a paddy wagon was waiting. A policeman opened the door and pushed Louis inside with other Black boys going to the Home.

Several years before, the men of New Orleans had realized that jail was no place for boys. Thinking that boys could be saved if given love, care, and guidance, Captain Joseph Jones and other men created a home for boys who were facing jail. Usually the boys were being jailed for minor offenses. Captain Jones and his men felt that real jail might turn the boys into true criminals.

Taking three abandoned buildings, Captain Jones and his crew begged lumber, paint, and supplies to restore these old buildings to use. Volunteers gave what was needed to complete the task.

One building was the dormitory where the boys spent most of their time. The next building was the chapel. The third building was the school. They took classes four days a week.

The home was managed by Captain Joseph Jones and his wife. Captain Jones was pleasant but strict, and his wife had a motherly smile. The

Joneses and all their helpers were Black.

When the paddy wagon reached the Waifs' Home, Captain and Mrs. Jones came out to meet the boys. Mrs. Jones took Louis by the hand and said, "This is your new home, young man. We hope you will like it here."

Louis pulled away his hand. He didn't answer Mrs. Jones.

Captain Jones noticed Louis' behavior and took him to one side. "We don't tolerate rudeness around here," he said. "When Mrs. Jones attempted to make you welcome, you jerked your hand away and didn't answer her."

Mrs. Jones had walked over to Louis' side. "I'm sorry, Ma'am, for being rude," he said. "Thank you for being nice to me. I'll try to be happy here."

Captain Jones took Louis to his office. "I need to ask you a few questions," he said. "Is Louis Armstrong your full name?"

"No, sir, my full name is Daniel Louis Armstrong," replied Louis.

"How old are you?" asked the Captain.

"I'm thirteen years old," answered Louis. "I was born July 4, 1900."

"Where do you live?" inquired the Captain.

"I've been living with my mother, Mayann Armstrong, in Brick Row," explained Louis.

114

"She's a hard-working woman who has given me a good home."

"How much schooling have you had?"

"I have finished the fifth grade," replied Louis. "I quit school to go to work to help my mother."

"Well, you will be required to go to school here," explained the Captain. "We teach reading, spelling, writing, and figuring. We also teach music, including singing, orchestra, and band. Then we have vocational training to help boys prepare for work when they grow up. We want all our boys to lead happy, successful lives. Now, do you have any questions?"

"Just one," replied Louis. "How long will I have to stay here?"

"There's no way of telling," explained Captain Jones. "Much will depend on your behavior. You certainly have to stay until you learn to live within the law."

Captain Jones arose, walked around to Louis,

and patted him on the shoulder. "Now let's go out to meet some of the boys," he said.

By now it was lunchtime at the home. Captain Jones led the way to a big dining room, where dozens of boys were seated at long tables. When Captain Jones and Louis reached the door, the Captain called out, "Boys, this is Louis Armstrong, who has come to live with us."

"Hello, Louis," called the group of boys. "Welcome to your new home."

Louis smiled weakly and sat down at one of the tables. He stared at the plate of food which was placed before him. Finally he pushed the plate away, wondering how he could ever get used to living away from his mother's home.

Already Captain Jones was determined to do something for Louis. He realized that Louis was a boy of the streets but felt that he had received good family training. He looked upon Louis' shooting escapade as more of a mistake than a crime. He regarded Louis basically as a good boy rather than as a bad boy deserving punishment.

The one thing that Louis felt he might become interested in here was music. The music teacher was Peter Davis, who was reluctant to accept Louis. He knew that Louis came from Brick Row, a section which many people called "bucket of blood" because so much needless blood was shed there.

During the first few days Louis hung around Mr. Davis, hoping to get his attention, but Mr. Davis completely ignored him. Gradually he gave up and concluded that he had little chance to learn music here.

From Bugler
to Saxophonist

THE LONGER Louis stayed at the Waifs' Home, the more homesick he became for his mother and sister. He felt that he never could be happy living in this strange place. Every day he wandered off by himself to keep from mingling with the other boys at the home.

All the while Captain Jones watched him very closely. He noticed how lonely and unhappy he was and wanted to do something to help him. At last he decided to find out what, if anything, he could do for him. He found him sitting all by himself in a corner of the yard. "Come, son," he said. "What's on your mind?"

Louis was touched by the sympathetic tone of Captain Jones's voice. He looked up and said, "I'm worried about my mother and sister. I just sit here and wonder how they are getting along without my help."

"Without your help?" asked Captain Jones.

"Yes, in daytime I've been driving a coal cart and helping a junk man," explained Louis. "Then at night I've been singing in a quartet to earn extra money. Sometimes I have been able to take my mother over two dollars from what I have earned in a day."

"That's fine," exclaimed Captain Jones, waiting for Louis to continue.

"Last week I bought my mother a new dress, the first she has had in several years," added Louis proudly. "And, sir, I earned all the money for the dress myself."

"What kind of work does your mother do to earn money?" asked Captain Jones.

"She never had any schooling, so she has to do such work as washing, ironing, cleaning, and cooking," replied Louis. "Now that I'm cooped up here, I don't know how she'll get along."

"Well, while you're here you can go to school and prepare to earn more money when you get out," explained Captain Jones. "We have a good job training program here."

"Yes, I know," said Louis, "but I'm homesick. I just want to go home."

Louis looked as if he might be going to cry. Then suddenly he surprised Captain Jones by asking, "Why do people call you Captain? Were you ever in the army?"

"Yes, I served in the army both in the West Indies and in the Philippines," replied Captain Jones proudly.

"I never heard of those places," said Louis, "but once I was a sergeant in a play army with a gang of boys here in New Orleans."

"Well, I was a sergeant in a real army, and I fought in a war," said Captain Jones.

"No fooling?" cried Louis, opening his eyes wide. He was really interested.

"In your history lessons here you will learn about wars," added Captain Jones. "I was a volunteer in the 9th Infantry during the Spanish-American War, and later I was a member of the Regular Army in the Philippines."

"Please tell me a little about the Spanish-American War," said Louis, moving closer to catch every word.

Captain Jones now could see that Louis really wanted to hear more, and he was happy to explain more fully. "To the south of our country," he went on, "there is a group of islands called the West Indies. Some of these islands, including Cuba and Puerto Rico, once were ruled by Spain. Our country had a battleship, called the *Maine*, anchored in a harbor in Cuba. Unexpectedly the Spanish forces blew up this battle-ship, killing many men. Then our country declared war on Spain."

"That sounds like something really serious," said Louis, listening intently.

"Yes, indeed, it was serious," said Captain Jones. "In order to protect ourselves from further trouble with Spain, we had to drive the Spanish forces out of the West Indies."

"How long did the war last?" asked Louis.

"Only a few months," replied Captain Jones. "Our troops invaded Cuba and charged up a hill to seize a fort, called Santiago. Then when they reached the top of the hill, the Spanish forces waved a white flag."

"Did waving the white flag mean that they were ready to give up?" asked Louis, his eyes wide with excitement.

"Yes, the Spanish forces surrendered, and the war soon ended," replied the Captain.

By now Captain Jones had won Louis' respect, but he kept on talking. "A few months later I joined the Regular Army and was sent to the Philippines, which we also had captured from Spain," he said. "While I was there, I was a bugler in the army. I played a bugle to tell the men when to get up in the morning and when to go to bed at night."

"Golly!" exclaimed Louis. "You must have felt important blowing that bugle."

"I guess I did, but I also learned much about music," continued Captain Jones. "After I returned home, I drilled a group of men in a drum and bugle corps. Some of these men started to call me Captain, and the name has stuck with me ever since."

Suddenly Captain Jones had an idea. He turned to Louis and asked, "How would you like to learn to play a bugle and become our bugler here at the Waifs' Home?"

"Oh, thank you, but do you think I can learn to play a bugle?" said Louis haltingly.

"Why, of course you can," replied Captain Jones. "Meet me here again after dinner."

Just then the dinner bell rang, and Louis rushed for the dining hall. "Gee, Captain Jones, you're great," he called back. "I'm as hungry as a bear."

Louis eagerly took his place at a table. Then right after grace was said, he tore into his plate of food. Captain Jones watched from a distance, now sure Louis' loneliness was over. Mrs. Jones watched, too, as she looked over and gave Louis a motherly smile.

After dinner Captain Jones came with a bugle. Louis started to practice at once, and later he became bugler at the Waifs' Home. He blew the bugle to let the boys know when to get up in the morning and when to go to bed at night. He felt very important with this assignment.

Almost immediately Louis began to enjoy living at the home. He still was eager to see his mother and sister, but soon they were allowed to come to see him regularly. From then on he was completely happy here. He felt that the Waifs' Home was a second home and that Mrs. Jones was a second mother.

Here at the home he no longer took the little black pills and pluto water which he had taken before. Instead, he lined up with the other boys once a week and took medicine under Mrs. Jones's direction. Very few of the boys ever became ill.

One evening after Louis had finished blowing the bugle, Captain Jones came to him and said, "You are doing a fine job for us, Louis. How do you like being a bugler?"

"Fine, sir," answered Louis. "I love it."

"Well, I think the time has come to add to your duties," said Captain Jones. "Up to now we

126

have been using a whistle to call the boys to meals, classes, sports, games, and other activities. From now on we'll let you blow a bugle to call them."

Captain Jones took another bugle and demonstrated several calls. Then Louis took the bugle and blew them almost perfectly after him. "I could tell that you have music in your soul," said Captain Jones, patting him affectionately on the shoulder.

Louis examined the bugle and noticed that the brass was dirty and green from age. He decided to give it a good polishing, and when he finished it was gleaming bright. He practiced standing erect and putting the bugle to his lips. He practiced blowing it to bring out its mellow tones. Suddenly he seemed to be living in a different world. He felt wanted, needed, and important. He never had been happier in his life.

Gradually as Mr. Davis observed Louis, he

came to have more respect for him. He was pleased with the way in which Louis played the bugle. Finally one day he smiled at Louis and said, "I like the way you blow the bugle."

Louis beamed at this remark. "Thank you, sir," he said, bowing politely.

Mr. Davis was impressed with Louis' gracious response. Already he had come to realize that Louis had musical talent. Suddenly he asked, "How would you like to play in our brass band here at Waifs' Home?"

Louis was so surprised by this question that he just stood speechless and stared at Mr. Davis. Then Mr. Davis repeated the question.

"Oh, thank you, sir," said Louis, recovering from his surprise. "Why, of course I would like to play in the band."

"Then come to rehearsal right after dinner," said Mr. Davis, moving quietly away.

After supper Louis washed up and rushed to

128

the rehearsal. All the members greeted him as if they were glad to have him join them. They felt that he had ability and would make a valuable addition to the band.

Louis had hoped that Mr. Davis would give him some kind of horn to play in the band. He was greatly disappointed when he was given a tambourine, but right away he started to practice. For years he had beat out rhythms on his knees, but now he had an opportunity to beat out rhythms on a real musical instrument. Soon Mr. Davis noted his enthusiasm for rhythm and switched him to playing drums. Now he could beat out rhythm to his heart's content.

A short time later, Mr. Davis needed an alto saxophone player in the band. Finally he surprised Louis by asking, "How would you like to learn to play an alto saxophone?"

Mr. Davis didn't wait for Louis to answer but handed him the saxophone. Louis took the instrument and said, "Thank you, Mr. Davis. I'll do the best I can, but someday I would like to learn to play a cornet."

Louis started in right away to master the new instrument. He practiced hard and was helped by his years of singing. Already he knew many of the melodies and soon could play along with the others. He liked the saxophone, but all the while he kept hoping that his next instrument would be a cornet.

Leader of Waifs' Home Band

"HELLO, LOUIS," said Captain Jones one day just as Louis had finished blowing his bugle. "You are doing a fine job on this assignment, and I'm very proud of you."

"Thank you, sir," said Louis as he brought the bugle down to his side.

"How are you doing in the band?" asked Captain Jones.

"Very well, I think," replied Louis with a broad grin. "I'm playing a saxophone, but I really would like to play a cornet. Unfortunately all the cornets are taken."

Captain Jones stood silently for a few moments in deep thought. Finally he said, "I just happened to think that I have an old cornet, but it doesn't look like much. Would you like to see it and try it out?"

Louis' eyes lighted up with excitement. "You bet I would," he replied. "When?"

"Right now," replied Captain Jones. "Just wait here while I go to get it."

Louis could hardly wait for Captain Jones to return. He was so excited when he saw him coming with the cornet that he ran to meet him. "Let's go far back in the yard, where we'll be all alone," said Captain Jones.

They went to the corner of the yard where they often met. Louis put the mouthpiece to his lips and tried to get the "feel" of the cornet. At first he had trouble holding the mouthpiece in place, because it was too small for his lips. Afterward he filed it to make it rough so he could hold it in place better.

In a half hour or so Louis could bring out all the sounds on the cornet, including the high ones. He knew that he would have to master these sounds before he could play real tunes. Captain Jones said proudly, "Just as I expected, you are starting off well. Take the cornet to band practice. Then possibly Mr. Davis will teach you to play a few melodies."

The next day Louis took the cornet to band practice and showed it to Mr. Davis. "Captain Jones let me have it," he explained. "Will you help me to learn to play it?"

"Certainly, Louis," replied Mr. Davis. By now he had come to have great respect for this boy from the notorious section of New Orleans. He took the cornet and proceeded to show Louis how to play "Home, Sweet Home." Later he showed him how to play several other familiar melodies. Louis was so thrilled that he practiced every spare moment of his time.

Soon Louis was able to play his cornet regularly in the band. With each practice period he played better and better. Mr. Davis greatly admired him for his skill. Suddenly one day he called Louis aside and said, "How would you like to become leader of the band?"

At first Louis was stunned. He could scarcely believe his ears and was too surprised to answer. Finally he managed to say, "Do you mean leader of the whole band?"

"Yes, I mean leader of the whole band," replied Mr. Davis.

"Well, that sounds great, but do you think I'm good enough?" asked Louis doubtfully.

"Yes, I'm sure, Louis," replied Mr. Davis "Besides, you learn very fast."

"Thank you, sir," cried Louis, jumping straight up in the air. At once he ran to tell Captain Jones about this new honor. He felt grateful to the Captain for giving him a start.

The band included twenty boys. They wore colorful uniforms made up of caps with black and white bands, blue gabardine coats, long white pants turned up at the bottom to look like knickers, black stockings, and black tennis shoes. Louis, as the leader, wore a cream-colored cap, a brown coat, cream-colored pants, brown stockings, and brown tennis shoes.

The band received many invitations to take part in parades on the streets of New Orleans and to play at celebrations and picnics. Louis looked forward to the time when the band would parade or play in his old neighborhood. He was eager for his mother and sister and all his friends to see that he had an important position in the band. He decided not to tell his mother and sister about being promoted to leader. Then later they would be surprised to see him strutting down the street.

Finally the band was invited to take part in

an important parade that would pass through Louis' old neighborhood. The boys had to march a long distance, but they didn't mind. They were excited and marched merrily along, strutting every step and playing like mad. Louis proudly marched in front, leading the way.

At first the people in Louis' old neighborhood didn't know what band was coming. When they saw Louis proudly leading the band, they crowded the sidewalks and started to cheer wildly. Mama Lucy ran fast to get her mother, who was still sleeping because she had worked late the night before. Little did she expect to see Louis come by, leading the Waifs' Home Band.

Amid cheers from the crowd, Louis led the band directly to a spot in front of his mother's home. Then he had the members play until she came out with Mama Lucy. At once the crowd made a place for them down front.

Tears ran down Mayann's cheeks as she stood

and listened to the band. "Thank the Lord," she said quietly to herself. "Now Louis will have a chance to do something with his life."

"What did you say?" asked a friend who was standing close beside her.

"I just thanked the Lord for helping Louis," she said. "I surely am proud to see him leading this band."

"The rest of us are, too," said the woman. "Louis belongs to all of us." With these words she walked over to Mr. Davis and asked, "May we take up a little collection for Louis?"

Mr. Davis agreed, and several boys passed hats in the crowd. Mr. Davis thought they would collect only a few pennies, but they collected several dollars. Louis gave the money to Mr. Davis to use for the band. From then on Louis frequently obtained permission to return home to visit his mother and sister.

Young Musician in New Orleans

LOUIS LIVED in the Colored Waifs' Home for Boys about a year and a half. Then he was released to his mother, who had often come to see him while he was there. When the time came to leave, Captain Jones, Mr. Davis, and all the boys shook hands with him to bid him good-by. Mrs. Jones kissed him affectionately and gave him a warm hug. He almost cried as he hurried away. He was afraid to look back.

For a short time after he left, he went to live with his father, whom he hadn't seen since he was a baby, and his stepmother, whom he had never seen at all. They lived in a little three-room house not far from where his mother and sister lived. Both his father and stepmother worked and he had to stay at home to take care of his two little half-brothers. Soon after he started to cook meals for them, he discovered that they had huge appetites. They ate so much that he had a hard time getting enough to eat himself. Finally he learned to hold back a little food whenever he served them.

Before long he had an opportunity to go back to live with his mother Mayann and his sister Mama Lucy. His stepmother had a baby girl, and there wasn't enough room in the house for six people to live comfortably. Besides, his father didn't earn enough money on his job to support such a large family.

Once Louis was settled back with his mother, he hoped to get a job playing in a band. One day he happened to meet an old friend who knew much about the cafes and dance halls in the neighborhood. "Do you know where I can get a job playing in a band?" he asked.

"Are you a cornet player?" asked his friend.

"Yes," replied Louis, "but I don't have a horn. The cornet which I formerly played belonged to Captain Jones."

"Well, there's an opening for a cornet player at the dance hall across the street," explained his friend, "but you'll have to wear long pants and act grown up. If you can get a horn, I think I can get you the job."

"Find out and let me know," said Louis. "I'll get a horn somewhere."

The next day Louis' friend reported that he could have the job. Now Louis had to find a way to earn money to rent a horn. He got a job driving a coal cart to haul coal to people's homes. He delivered an average of five loads a day and was paid fifteen cents a load. Soon he saved enough money to rent a cornet.

At once he started to play at the dance hall, but decided to keep his steady job with the coal company. He drove the coal cart during the day and caught a few hours sleep before he reported to the dance hall in the evening. Each night at the dance hall he earned one dollar and a quarer plus tips. Many people gave him tips to play special tunes for them.

Regularly Louis took money home to his mother and sister, but soon he saved enough from tips to buy an old nickel-plated cornet. Now he felt more independent with his own cornet, but he still kept his job driving the coal cart. His friends couldn't understand why he kept this job now that he was playing in a band. "Well, it's always a good thing to have a steady job," explained Louis. "You never can tell when the dance hall might close."

Louis' thinking was right. Before long the dance hall closed. Now he was glad that he had kept the coal job. He still managed to take a little money home to his mother.

A short time later he obtained a job playing in a much better band. At first he received very little pay, but he soon was raised to one dollar and twenty-five cents per night, which was top pay at that time. All the while he kept on driving the coal cart.

While he held these two jobs, he and his mother and sister led very happy lives. His mother, who was an excellent cook, prepared many fine meals for him and Mama Lucy to eat. She even taught both of them to cook some of their own favorite dishes.

During this period World War I had started in Europe and many people were afraid our country would be forced to enter the war. The attendance at dance halls dropped off and musicians earned less. Then Louis saved carefully for a time when he might be out of work.

Formerly at New Orleans it was customary to have bands play at funerals, but Louis had never played at a funeral. In fact, he had never attended a funeral except the one years before for Sally Lee's husband. Finally one of Louis' teenage friends died, and young people chipped in to hire a brass band to play at the funeral. They selected the Onward Brass Band, which included some of the finest musicians in New Orleans. One was Joe "King" Oliver, who played a cornet.

After the funeral services in the church, the Onward Brass Band played softly "Nearer My God to Thee" to lead the funeral procession to the cemetery. The mourners, many in tears, marched along behind the band. As Louis marched with the others, he came to realize that death was real and that it was final.

At the cemetery the band continued to play "Nearer My God to Thee," but more softly than before. The mourners stood with bowed heads as the body was lowered into the grave. Then the preacher solemnly uttered the words, "Ashes to ashes and dust to dust," and offered a final prayer.

There was a brief pause following the prayer, after which the band marched out into the street and struck up a rousing tune, "Didn't He Ramble?" Then it led the way back toward town, with people swaying along behind. Many new people joined the crowd on the way to town. These new people who followed along behind were called the second line.

Louis was impressed with the music at his friend's funeral and decided that he would like to play at funerals. He knew that some of the leading musicians in the city, including King Oliver, played in funeral bands. He wanted an opportunity to play with Oliver and other important musicians. Finally the opportunity came and he had a chance to play with King Oliver. At once they became close friends.

At this time King Oliver was the top trumpet player at a night club. After he became interested in Louis, he began to teach him how to read music and how to play a trumpet. From then on he called Louis "Little Louis" and Louis called him "Papa Joe."

The attendance at dance halls was still low, and Louis had little opportunity to play in bands except at funerals. Finally in 1917 the newspapers of New Orleans and all parts of the country carried the following headlines:

UNITED STATES DECLARES WAR ON GERMANY
"The world must be made safe for democracy—"
President Wilson

Louis was not sure what these headlines meant, but he knew that men were being drafted into the army and navy. Posters about town showed Uncle Sam pointing a finger at young men and saying, "I want you." Louis looked at these posters and thought that they meant him, too. He tried to enlist but was too young.

During the war many soldiers and sailors were trained in the vicinity of New Orleans. When they were off duty, they flocked to dance halls for entertainment. The government disapproved and ordered many dance halls closed.

After the dance halls were closed, musicians had a hard time making a living. King Oliver, who then was playing trumpet in Kid Ory's band, left and went to Chicago. The band continued, however, and Louis took his place. Soon he built up great popularity for his ability to improvise or add all sorts of new tones in a melody. Later he obtained a job playing in a popular restaurant in New Orleans.

Finally after World War I ended in 1918, Louis was doing so well that he decided to get

married. He married a young lady named Daisy, and at once they began to have problems. She had no particular love for music and couldn't understand why he couldn't do other work in order to spend more time at home. By now, however, he knew that he couldn't give up music because it was the thing he knew best. It was the thing he could do best.

After a year Louis and Daisy decided to separate, but they parted as friends. Daisy couldn't develop any love for music or any pride in Louis' popularity as a musician. On the other hand, Louis now was so wrapped up in music that he couldn't think of dropping it. The friendly separation turned into a divorce, and each one went their separate ways permanently.

After Louis and Daisy divorced, he took a job playing in an orchestra on a Mississippi River excursion steamboat called the *Dixie Belle*. This steamboat left New Orleans in the early evening

149

and returned about midnight. The passengers on board danced to the music and had gay times. Later Louis obtained better jobs playing in orchestras on steamboats that traveled long distances up and down the Mississippi River. Some of these steamboats went as far north as St. Louis, Missouri.

While Louis was playing on steamboats, he wrote one of his first songs. He called the song "Get Off Katie's Head," but the publishers chose to call it "I Wish I Could Shimmy Like My Sister Kate." This first song was only one of many that he composed during his lifetime. Now he was a composer as well as a musician.

Early Days in Chicago

IN THE FALL of 1921, after Louis had spent the summer playing on an excursion boat, he took a job playing in a cabaret. Also, whenever possible, he played at funerals about the city. One day when he had just returned from playing at a funeral, he received the following telegram from King Oliver in Chicago:

I WANT YOU TO COME UP AND JOIN ME.
PAPA JOE

"Are you going?" asked the tuba player.

"Sure, I'm going," replied Louis.

"But you have a steady job here," argued the

tuba player. "Just think of all the persons who go to Chicago to get jobs and have to hobo their way back. It might happen to you."

"Papa Joe is my friend," replied Louis. "All my life was wrapped up in him before he left for Chicago. His wanting me to join him is the biggest thing that could happen to me. Yes, I'm going. I have to."

Louis' mother and sister were shocked about his leaving. They bade him good-by at home because they couldn't bear to go to the railroad station. "Put on your long underwear, so you won't catch cold up north," cautioned his mother. "And be careful to keep out of trouble with those big city slickers."

"Aw, Mama, don't worry," Louis assured her. "I'll be all right up there with Papa Joe."

"Yes, I know," said his mother. "This is a big break for you. You were born to make people happy with your music and your smile."

Sadly the members of the Tuxedo Brass Band went to the railroad station to see Louis off. With tears in their eyes they waved as the train pulled away on its long trip north.

When Louis got off the train in Chicago, he looked about the station for Papa Joe, but couldn't find him. He attracted much attention as he walked about wearing a double-breasted suit with padded shoulders and wide-legged pants. He wore a wide-brimmed hat and carried a straw suitcase. At first when Papa Joe failed to meet him at the station, he was tempted to take the first train back to New Orleans. Then suddenly a redcap walked up to him and asked, "Are you Louis Armstrong?"

"Yes," replied Louis in great surprise.

"Well, King Oliver wants me to bring you to the Royal Gardens," explained the redcap.

When they reached the Royal Gardens, Louis noticed a big sign in front which read, "Oliver's

Original Creole Band." Briefly he stood watching and listening to the band play and said, "One thing is sure. It's too good for me."

As Louis hung back, King Oliver came over and grabbed him. "Come in here, Little Louis," he exclaimed. "I need you."

"O.K., Papa Joe," grinned Louis, following him to the spot where the band was seated.

"This is Little Louis," Oliver said, and the members of the band started to laugh.

"They surely grow little boys big down south," said the drummer jokingly.

Louis took out his horn and joined the band, and everybody seemed to be pleased with his playing. That night Papa Joe took him home with him to stay all night. His wife Stella was happy to see Louis and welcomed him like a son.

The next afternoon King Oliver arranged a rehearsal so that Louis could learn to play with the band. Oliver played lead cornet, and Louis played second cornet. They blended their two horns well together, just as King Oliver had known they would from the beginning.

As Louis looked over the band, he was impressed with a four thousand dollar ring which the clarinet player flashed from one of his fingers. Even more, however, he was attracted by the cute little piano player, Lil Hardin.

"How do you like him, Lil?" asked King Oliver as the band rested from practice.

Lil Hardin merely shrugged her shoulders as if to say, "so, so." Actually she hadn't paid any attention to Louis.

Earlier that week Lil had purchased an automobile. Now she was especially eager for the rehearsal to end so she could practice driving. Finally she said, "Let's call it a day. I'll take you and Louis for a ride."

"We're game to accept," said King Oliver, winking slyly at Louis.

Lil was short, petite, and active, but somewhat independent. She had been reared in a fine home where she had been allowed to have her own way. She had started her musical training at Fisk University in Nashville, Tennessee, and had obtained her degree in music at Chicago. She had no expenses at home and could buy whatever she wanted, particularly attractive clothes and now an automobile.

As a young adult Lil had many friends, but she never had had a real romance. She loved music and had always let it dominate her life. She was lively, enjoyed the fun of living, and made persons around her happy.

When Lil and her two passengers, King Oliver and Louis, reached her automobile, she hopped in the front seat behind the wheel. Then she flipped her head and motioned for them to get in the back seat. "Climb in and relax," she said gaily. "This ride should be fun."

Both men climbed in and sat on the back seat as Lil had directed. King Oliver seemed relaxed, but Louis felt a bit nervous, because he had ridden in cars only three times before. All his life in New Orleans he had either walked or ridden in a trolley car.

Lil pulled away from the curb and started to drive along Michigan Avenue, one of the leading streets in the city. All went well until she had to stop for traffic at a cross street. Then the motor died and she couldn't get it started again. King Oliver and Louis became tickled by her impatience and started to giggle. "Okay, you smart guys," she cried. "Come up and drive."

Louis' eyes opened wide with embarrassment. "I'm sorry, but I can't drive," he said. "I've only been in three cars in my life."

"I can't drive either," admitted King Oliver half apologetically. "All I can do is sit back and ride when someone else is driving."

By now Lil became amused and broke into hearty laughter. She and the two men climbed out of the car to get help. Soon they stopped a passing motorist. "My motor has stopped," explained Lil, "and I need help to get it started."

The man raised the hood of the car and soon discovered the difficulty. He made a few adjustments and asked Lil to try to start the motor again. It started perfectly and she thanked him for his help. During the remainder of the afternoon she gave King Oliver and Louis a delightful ride about the city.

After this early meeting Lil and Louis began to pal around together during coffee breaks. She frequently looked in his direction and smiled as she sat at the piano. In return he broke into a big grin or as much of one as he could while playing his cornet.

Soon after Louis' arrival, King Oliver arranged for the band to make its first record.

During the recording he decided that Louis was playing too loudly and had him move several feet away. Lil noticed what King Oliver had done and asked him about it. "Why did you move Louis back during the recording?" she asked.

"Frankly, because he can play better than I can," said Oliver. "I had to move him to keep his playing from overshadowing mine."

At once she became worried. She wanted Louis to succeed and was afraid that King Oliver might hold him back. She realized that King Oliver was playing first cornet and Louis only second cornet, but she wanted Louis to have a chance to play his best. Since she was a fixer, she decided that somehow she would have to solve this problem. Louis must not be held back.

Stardom in Chicago

ONE EVENING at the dinner table King Oliver and his wife Stella had a heart-to-heart talk about Louis. Both of them loved him as a son. They had come to know him as a growing boy in New Orleans and could scarcely realize that he now was a full-grown man. "He's just a country boy hitting the big city for the first time," said King Oliver. "It won't be good for him to advance too rapidly."

"You're right," replied Stella, "but remember you can't keep him with you forever. He really has musical talent, and you must let him make his own mark in the world."

"Of course I will when the time comes," agreed King Oliver. "I need him, but I won't hold him back. When he gets a good opportunity to play elsewhere, I'll let him go."

Stella walked around to her husband's side and gently kissed him on the cheek. "Don't worry about Louis any more," she said. "You notice that he isn't here for dinner tonight."

For a moment King Oliver sat staring into space. "I don't quite understand," he said. "What are you trying to tell me?"

"Simply that Louis is having dinner with Lil tonight," explained Stella. "He told me and asked whether I needed anything before he left. It's nice to have him around. He takes the place of the son that we never had."

"We'll probably lose him to Lil," said King Oliver. "The two of them are sort of together. Lil is little and bossy, always telling him what to do or shaking her finger at him to get him to do something. In return, he just looks at her adoringly and tries to do exactly what she wants him to do."

"I know," said Stella. "Now she wants him to wear better clothes. She wants him to stop wearing second-hand clothes and buy new clothes at a store. Furthermore, she wants him to learn to handle his own money."

"I guess that's part of growing up," said King Oliver. "He always has been used to somebody helping him look after his money. Lil is no spendthrift. She'll see that he spends wisely for things that he needs."

"Now that he has taken up with her," said Stella, "we'll probably see less of him."

"Yes, that's to be expected," agreed King Oliver, "but she will be good for him. She's a real musician with a college degree in music. Sooner or later Louis will go out on his own in music, but I'll always love him like a son."

One afternoon Louis and Lil went to a motion picture show together. They had about a half hour to wait before it was time to start playing for the evening. "You're really a lot of fun to be with," said Lil.

"What do you enjoy about being with a country boy like me?" asked Louis seriously. "The fellows all say that you never were particularly interested in any man before."

Lil was surprised by this question. She paused to look at him in his new clothes, which fitted him. "Well, I just need someone to boss, and you seem to take my bossing real well," she said. Then they both laughed.

Moments later Louis and Lil happily joined the band for the evening performance. King Oliver winked at the other players, who readily saw that a romance was on the way. About six months later Louis and Lil were married.

King Oliver and Stella were very happy about

the marriage, but realized that Lil soon would want Louis to move up and become a star. "Louis is just too good to stay in my band any longer," said King Oliver. "Actually, I'm holding him back and Lil knows it. It's only a matter of time until he'll leave."

Finally the break came. Through Lil Louis had an opportunity to play first trumpet in a band at the Dreamland in Chicago. "I hate to leave Papa Joe," he said.

"I know," replied Lil, "but you have to look out for yourself."

"Just remember that Papa Joe brought me here and still needs me," argued Louis. "It doesn't seem right for me to leave him."

"Look, Louis, you're a great player," said Lil in a determined tone of voice, "but you won't get any place until you can play as you want. You know all the tricks with a horn, but you can't display them as long as you play second cornet for Papa Joe. There's no other way. You just have to get out on your own."

Louis loved Lil and respected her ability in music. He realized that she knew many things about music that he didn't know. Finally he decided to have a good talk with Papa Joe. He told him about his new offer. "Lil thinks I should take it and get out on my own," he explained. "What do you think, Papa Joe?"

King Oliver was prepared. He was hurt, but he had expected this day to come. "This may be your big break, Louis," he said. "I've had many breaks, but I have a cataract on one eye and may be nearing the end of my career. If you have a chance to move up, take it."

"I'm not interested in moving up, Papa Joe," replied Louis. "I don't want to become a big star. I'm happy with you, and I would just like to stay on with you forever."

"Some people are born to be big and some to

be little," continued King Oliver. "You were born to be big. Just don't fight it."

"Please don't tell me that," pleaded Joe. "I don't want to be big."

"But you should," argued Papa Joe. "You're married to Lil. She knows music and the right people. She knows how to get you into the right spots. Don't hold back any longer."

"I'll never forget you, Papa Joe," said Louis, rising to leave. "You surely have been a father to me when I needed you."

"I'm glad," replied King Oliver with tears in his eyes. "Now most of all I want you to look out for the breaks."

Louis took the job at the Dreamland, but Lil soon learned that a noted band leader in New York needed a trumpet player. At her insistence Louis tried out for the job and won. While he was in New York he helped to make a number of records. Once while he was recording a song, he accidentally dropped his music. Immediately he began to improvise, singing mere sounds instead of words. This new type of singing, called "scat" singing, attracted wide attention.

After Louis had spent a year in New York, he returned to Chicago to play lead cornet in a little band which Lil had organized to play at the Sunset Cafe. This cafe was owned and operated by Joe Glaser, who was destined some years later to become Louis' business manager. The following announcement about the new band appeared in a Chicago *Black Weekly:*

Lil Hardin's Dreamland Syncopaters
Featuring
World's Greatest Jazz Cornetist
Louis Armstrong

Louis was a great success. The crowds poured in. Lil beamed. This was the greatest break Louis had ever had, but soon King Oliver, who led a band in a nearby cafe, needed a trumpet player. At once Louis was torn between keeping his present fine position or returning to play for King Oliver. "Why should you want to go back?" asked Lil in amazement.

"Because I'm not happy away from Papa Joe," replied Louis. "Somehow I feel more comfortable by his side."

"But you can't always lean on Papa Joe," argued Lil impatiently. "You'll just have to learn to lean on yourself."

Following this discussion, they decided that Louis should talk once more with Papa Joe. He told Papa Joe that he was making a good salary, but that he wanted to be back with him. "I'm not happy away from you," he said.

Again Papa Joe stood his ground. "You're much better off where you are," he argued. "You're on your way up. Don't fight it."

Louis continued at the Sunset Cafe, where his name flashed in bright lights over the entrance. Finally through Lil he had an opportunity to join a fifteen-piece orchestra at the Vendome Theater. He could take this job and continue to play at the Sunset Cafe, because he would play at different hours. "I just can't accept it," he said to Lil, "because I've never played that kind of music before."

"But you must," insisted Lil. "Playing there will be good for you. Just remember that you can read music and play a great horn."

"Well, I'll try it," replied Louis, "but who wants to be bothered with reading music, turning sheets, and all such stuff?"

In the meantime crowds continued to pour in at the Sunset Cafe to hear Louis play. Lil wanted him to stand on the stage while he played, but he continuously refused. Finally she had a spotlight turned on him at his station in the band. At first he felt very uncomfortable, but finally became used to it.

170

Many famous white musicians and even composers came to hear and watch Louis perform. They studied his mannerisms, his many musical tricks, and his appealing type of improvising. Then they borrowed some of them.

Gradually as the crowds continued to increase at the Sunset Cafe, the attendance fell off at the nearby cafe where King Oliver was playing. Finally he decided to end his musical career and return to New Orleans. "I've been playing long enough," he said to Louis. "Besides, my eyes have been bothering me more and more. Now Stella and I can go back home in New Orleans. You're on your way up. Just keep going."

In 1927 Louis received word that his mother Mayann was ill. At once he and Lil traveled to New Orleans to see her. For years he had sent her money and urged her to come to live with them in Chicago, but she had refused. Now they hoped to take her home with them.

When they reached Louis' old neighborhood, Lil was impressed with his mother's neat little two-room house. She understood why his mother had been comfortable and happy here closely surrounded by friends.

As soon as they entered the house, Louis went over to the bed, kissed his mother, and introduced Lil. "I'm glad you have come," his mother said with a weak smile. "And I'm glad you have brought your wife to see me. Already I like her." She smiled at Lil and Louis beamed, happy to have his mother's approval.

"We've come to take you back to Chicago with us, Mama," said Louis after they had a short visit. "We want you to live with us."

At first Mayann objected, but finally consented to go. She lived only a short time in Chicago, but Louis and Lil were pleased to have had her. "I'm glad Mama got to know some of the good things of life before she died," said

Louis. "She always had a hard life. As a girl she worked from morning to night in cotton and sugar cane fields. After she grew up, she washed, ironed, cleaned, and cooked for people. She worked hard for Mama Lucy and me."

In 1928 Louis accepted a position to play at the Savoy Ballroom, one of the leading night spots in Chicago. By now, however, hard times were creeping across the country, and many Black people were losing their jobs. Finally in 1929 the stock market crashed, and the country slumped into a depression.

Louis now knew that there would be little opportunity for musicians in Chicago. Finally he decided to take his band to New York, where he hoped the outlook would be better. He and the members started out in four little automobiles, planning to put on shows along the way to help pay their expenses. Lil remained in Chicago, where she still had steady employment.

Climax of a Fabulous Career

ALMOST immediately when Armstrong and his band reached New York, they were booked to play at Connie's Inn on Broadway, in the heart of the theater district. While here Armstrong attracted wide attention by introducing his popular song, "Ain't Misbehavin'." This song, with words as follows, became a rage during the early years of the depression, when a great many people were out of work.

I don't stay out late, no place to go.
I'm home about eight, just me and my radio.
Ain't misbehavin'. I'm savin' my love for you.

After spending about a year in New York, Armstrong went on a musical tour of the United States, which ended up in Hollywood, California. There he and his band spent much of 1930, broadcasting and making records. Some of the tunes which he helped to make famous were: "Old Rockin' Chair's Got Me," "Chinatown," "Tiger Rag," "I Can't Give You Anything but Love," and "Struttin' with Some Barbecue."

In 1931 Armstrong and his band made another musical tour of the United States which ended up in his boyhood town of New Orleans. On this tour he introduced his popular hit song, "You Rascal, You." From New Orleans he made his first trip to Europe, where he discovered that people were fascinated with this same song hit. When he reached England, musicians and musical critics gave him a mammoth reception. One night while he was appearing in London, King George V and a party of friends came to hear him. During the performance, he bowed in the direction of the royal box and said, "This one is for you, Rex." The word "Rex" which he used is the Latin word for "King."

On this first trip to Europe Armstrong acquired the nickname "Satchmo." For years people had called him "Satchelmouth" because of his large mouth. In writing a story about Armstrong, the editor of a London magazine left out a few letters in the word Satchelmouth and shortened it to Satchmo. This shortened nickname stuck with Armstrong the rest of his life.

When Armstrong returned to America, this country was in the depth of the depression, with many people, including musicians, out of work. He cooperated with the Federal government in trying to find work for unemployed musicians. In addition, he loaned money to many of his musical friends.

In 1933 Armstrong and his band started an

extensive tour of Europe which lasted through the succeeding winter. On this tour he visited Denmark, Sweden, Norway, England, the Netherlands, Belgium, Switzerland, France, and Italy. Everywhere he went people turned out in hordes to hear him. He gave an average of three concerts a day, all of which were sellouts.

At Marseilles, France, a group of young musicians came two hundred miles to attend one of his concerts. When they arrived, they were deeply disappointed to find that all the seats had been sold. Armstrong shared their disappointment and arranged for them to stand in the wings off the stage to watch the concert. They were thrilled by his personal attention and thanked him profusely.

When Armstrong returned to America, he toured the United States briefly, and went back on Broadway. In the meantime Lil had continued to live in their home in Chicago. She even had purchased a summer home in Idle-wild, Michigan, which Louis had never seen. Now that he had become a world-famous musician, he never had time to stay in Chicago. As a result, he and Lil gradually drifted apart, each leading a busy life without the other.

In 1937 when Armstrong and his band were on a tour of the United States, they were booked to appear at Savannah, Georgia. While there he was surprised to find his old friend King Oliver running a vegetable stand in a market. "Hello, Papa Joe," he exclaimed. "What in the world are you doing here?"

King Oliver explained that after he and his wife Stella had left Chicago and returned to New Orleans, he couldn't obtain work as a musician. Before long she had died, leaving him alone in the world. Then during the depression he had taken whatever jobs he could get. After hearing this story, Armstrong reached in his pocket and handed Papa Joe all the money he had. He still loved him like a father.

That night at Armstrong's invitation, Papa Joe stood in the wings of the stage during the performance. He was thrilled to have an opportunity to attend a concert given by his former pupil and friend. After the concert, he and Armstrong visited and joked until far into the night. They parted tearfully.

A few months after this chance meeting in Savannah, King Oliver died suddenly of a heart attack. Armstrong was deeply grieved by the sad news. The first time he was in Chicago, he told Lil the gloomy story about the later years of King Oliver's life. "He was just a victim of hard luck and hard times," said Armstrong.

"Did he seem to be unhappy when you saw him?" asked Lil.

"No," replied Armstrong, "but I knew that he was just pretending. He displayed a wonderful spirit even though he had lost nearly everything he had valued in life."

"What an unfortunate way to end a career," said Lil with tears in her eyes.

"Yes, without doubt Papa Joe died of a broken heart," said Armstrong. "He had nothing left to do except to die. I'm certainly glad that I got to see him before he passed on."

From 1936 to 1966 Armstrong combined his musical career with a motion picture career. He started his movie career with the musical hit, "Pennies from Heaven." In suceeding years he starred in the following memorable musicals: "Every Day's a Holiday," "Going Places," "Dr. Rhythm," "Cabin in the Sky," "Jam Session," "New Orleans," "The Strip," "Glory Alley," "The Glenn Miller Story," "High Society," "The Five Pennies," and finally "A Man Called Adam."

During these years, Armstrong played, sang, and performed as a musical star. His brilliance plus his simple stage mannerisms endeared him everywhere he went. His greatest opportunity came when he was booked for the musical comedy "Hello, Dolly." His movie version of this comedy was shown millions of times before audiences in all parts of the world.

Early in Armstrong's expanding career, he chose his old friend Joe Glaser to become his business manager. Glaser had owned the Sunset Cafe in Chicago where Armstrong had played in Lil Hardin's band. He proved to be a very able and helpful manager as well as friend.

For years Louis and Lil had led separate careers. She had liked Chicago and he had become attached to New York. Finally they obtained a divorce but remained friends. Years later he married Lucille Wilson, a chorus girl whom he had met in New York. She became a very devoted helpmate who accompanied him on many of his extended tours.

Lucille Armstrong had her first opportunity to visit her husband's hometown in 1949 when he was invited to be King of the Annual Zulu Parade in New Orleans. This was a special parade for Black people which had been started to poke fun at the famous carnival, called Mardi Gras, held in New Orleans. It was sponsored by the Zulu Social Aid and Pleasure Club, a burial society composed entirely of Black people. This club had been formed to see that members who kept their dues paid would have decent burials when they died. In earlier days no insurance company would insure Black people.

Armstrong was the first Black person from New Orleans ever invited to lead the Zulu parade. When he received the invitation, he said, "All my life I've wanted to be King of the Zulu Parade. Now my chance has come. After this I'll be ready to die."

When the day arrived, Armstrong emerged

from a foggy bank of the Mississippi River, wearing a grass skirt over black-dyed underwear. He wore a silver crown on his head and had a green velvet cape with silver trimmings thrown over his shoulders. In his hand he carried a purple and gold spear.

As King he proudly boarded the first of the Zulu Parade floats. All along the parade route, he waved his spear and performed various sorts of antics to entertain the crowd. Hundreds of thousands of spectators packed the streets to watch and to cheer him.

The float stopped at shops and stores along the way to honor persons who had helped to pay for the parade. From time to time pages on the float tossed coconuts into the crowd. Altogether they threw two thousand coconuts at the merry revelers, who scrambled to get them.

Near the end of the parade the float collapsed and the crowd went wild with excitement.

When Armstrong was certain nobody was hurt, he took over with his natural showmanship to entertain the spectators. By joking and performing antics, he kept them roaring with laughter.

Although Armstrong was greeted in New Orleans by tumultuous applause, several Black organizations felt that the character of the King of Zulu Parade presented a warped picture of Black people in America. They complained that the Zulu Parade was a symbol of everything contrary to the hopes, aspirations, and desires of responsible Black citizens. Actually, however, most of the spectators looked upon the parade as a source of entertainment and fun and cared little about anything else.

Armstrong himself had considered the Zulu Parade merely as an opportunity for a home-town boy to return to entertain his relatives and friends. He had been proud to have his sister Mama Lucy and his half-brothers watching enthusiastically along with the others. When he was told about the criticism of his performance, he said, "To poke fun at yourself in no way robs you of your self-respect. Rather it gives you a sense of importance and security."

In future years Armstrong became more and more endeared to the people of the United States and the world. Many called him "Ambassador of Good Will" because he brought pleasure to all groups, regardless of nationality, color, or creed. He loved human beings everywhere and sought to make everybody happy.

In the later years of his life Armstrong made two memorable trips to Africa. On his first trip, when he reached Accra, Ghana, he was greeted by one hundred thousand cheering admirers. He made his second trip to Africa to conduct a cultural mission for the United States government. When he reached Leopoldville, Congo, in central Africa, his admirers carried him on a canvas throne to the huge meeting place where he was to appear. Everywhere he went people appreciated the colorful, rhythmic type of music they had come to associate with him.

In 1965 Armstrong barnstormed through Europe on a two-month tour, returning to many cities which he had visited before. Again people flocked to halls and stadiums to hear him and to see him. Everywhere he went he spread the spirit of good will.

During this same year a great celebration, called a "Salute to Louis Armstrong," was held in Carnegie Hall in New York City. This celebration was held to commemorate Armstrong's fifty years in show business. It brought together some of the leading bands, orchestras, singing groups, and soloists in the country, both Black and white. As a climax to the celebration, Senator Jacob Javits of New York, representing the government of the United States, presented

Armstrong with a plaque honoring him for the many missions which he had undertaken for our government in other countries. The program was televised so that millions of admirers could share in the tribute.

During the last two years of his life, Armstrong suffered ill health which kept him from playing with his band. He kept hoping to play again and even carried a mouthpiece in his pocket, which he used to keep his lips in shape. Whenever he was able, he practiced for short periods of time with his trumpet. He spent much of this time at home with his wife Lucille, the same home they had shared ever since their marriage. On July 6, 1971, he died suddenly, two days after his seventy-first birthday.

People everywhere were shocked to learn of his death. After fifty years in show business he had become one of the most popular entertainers in the world. In New York his wife invited five hundred former musical associates and friends to attend his funeral services. On the way to the cemetery the funeral procession passed along streets crowded with mourners, many in tears. At one point a group held up a large sign which read, "We all loved you, Louis."

Special memorial services were held for Armstrong in numerous cities across the country. A service in New Orleans was held only a few days after he died. It was held on the plaza in front of the City Hall, where a large crowd could assemble. Three jazz bands played along streets to lead mourners to the plaza. The services included a brief sermon and prayer by a local minister and a brief eulogy by the mayor. Then the three bands struck up the old familiar song, "When the Saints Go Marching In."

A few weeks later memorial services were held in Chicago in Grant Park, on the shore of Lake Michigan. One of those who took part in the services was Armstrong's former wife, Lillian Hardin Armstrong. During the ceremony she started to play "St. Louis Blues" as a piano solo. She played in her same old enthusiastic manner, rocking on the bench and tossing her hands up from the keys. Suddenly, midway through the selection, she fell face forward on the keyboard and died.

In January, 1972, a notable tribute was paid to Armstrong during the "Super Bowl" football game which was played at New Orleans by the Dallas Cowboys and the Miami Dolphins. At half-time in this world championship game, famous musicians entertained the spectators by playing and singing jazz music which Armstrong had helped to popularize during his lifetime. Besides those attending the game, millions enjoyed the tribute by television.

When Armstrong died in 1971, many of his former friends in New Orleans had preceded him in death, including Captain Joseph Jones, who had served as his foster father in the Colored Waifs' Home for Boys. Mrs. Jones, however, still lived and was deeply grieved to learn of his death.

Following Armstrong's death, Mrs. Jones released the following interesting comments: "Louis was a good boy. He followed directions, was dependable, and appreciated whatever a person did for him. When I saw him play his heart out on the old battered horn which my husband loaned him, I knew that he loved music. From this start he went on to become one of the world's greatest. Now I'm thankful that my husband and I were around to lend him a helping hand when he needed help."